Two Faces of Beauty

A Collection of Micro Didactics

William Davis

authorHOUSE®

AuthorHouse™
1663 Liberty Drive
Bloomington, IN 47403
www.authorhouse.com
Phone: 1 (800) 839-8640

Published by AuthorHouse 03/21/2016

ISBN: 978-1-5049-8611-3 (sc)
ISBN: 978-1-5049-8612-0 (e)

Print information available on the last page.

A Dedication

The goal and substance of micro didactics is the compression of the most possible knowledge, information and instruction into the fewest possible words. In this case its sources are the memories endowed me by the features of my universe, the sum of my learning experiences compacted into the following.

It stands to reason that the dedication must be to that source. A vast field of dreams, both awake and sleeping. To the countless, radically different people I have known. Also to the many varying and sometimes unbelievable events of my life.

So many years that now seem like so few. Many times I have soared high in my life and experienced the best the world can be. That contrast sharply with the times I have stood at death's door, struck down with despair as I witnessed universal dismay.

So many people lent their hands in my continued existence just as some have tried to end it. The lovers, the dear friends, the strangers that have reached out to me as I lay bloody and beaten, these individuals are a part of this work. But no more than the people that have oppressed me. The dangerous and bastardly hypocrites that hold positions of power. The close friend gone bad, the lying partner, those who would attack me with lies and those who would kill me from the shadows ... I owe all for all have shaped my world.

I will only descend into specifics to point to the one force, event, device, institution or person (in this case a person) that is most responsible for the creation of this work. That would be my wife, Mary.

So ... To the totality of the universe and to my beautiful woman this work is dedicated.

William Davis

Foreword

Having known William Davis for more than twenty years, I can attest to the somewhat demented imagination of this most prolific and talented writer. I have been the sounding board for many of his works, and I am seldom disappointed in what I read. Bill is the one who challenged me to write, and now I'm a published author with a few minor awards to my credit.

William Davis has won many awards and competitions with his unique and entertaining view on life, absurdities of life, and tragedies of life. You will laugh, cry, and sometimes be confused, but you will always be entertained.

Enjoy!

Jack Crowsey

Published Author

I must state first and foremost that I am proud to call Bill my friend. I have watched him wrestle with the forces he mentions in the introduction of this work and personally witnessed the effects of life-lessons God diligently bestowed on Bill. What marvelous works are we!

In complete honesty he watched me wrestle with some of those same forces—forces which very much shaped who I am today. I have learned that our value as a human being, like that of any piece of fine art, comes not from the intrinsic values of the piece, but from the identity of the Author or Artist…and for the last price paid for the work.

In that, we are without a doubt, valued beyond measure! No less can be said of my good friend, William H. Davis Jr.

Join him on his journey of discovery. You will not be disappointed!

K. Wayne MacKenzie

Author of *Regenerate: A Brief History of the Delta-Phi*

Introduction

The collection of tales before you so dubbed "Micro Didactics" consist of both fiction and non-fiction stories. Some of the work may not be immediately identifiable as either. All are a product of my turbulent childhood, my education, my reckless adult experiences and my neurotic afflictions.

These factors forged together in the fires of my inner most being and the results lay before you, the product of self-realization. Self-realization can be a great force for discovery.

But beware, what I discovered was sometimes ugly, disturbing and even evil. I discovered that I shared something in common with every character I created and even those I didn't. Despite this rather unsettling fact I believe myself to be better off.

Perhaps the reader will be lead to discover through self-realization.

Just as a man can elevate himself to being a child of God through belief, so can another man believe himself to be only the most evolved life form on earth and thereby reduce himself to an animal.

As a bullet is permanently and uniquely marked by the lands of the barrel it travels through, I was marked by the forces in my life that empowered me with the self-awareness that spilled out upon these pages in the form of micro didactics.

It is my most sincere hope that these bits of "micro didactics" will inspire self-realization for the betterment of the reader and the world.

Table of Contents

A Feral Love Story

From what I can make of the ancient cryptic markings this land was once called North America and it had many great colonies. I have seen the remains of the dwellings that reached to the sky in the place the cryptic markings call Cleveland. Once after I was a man and a scout for the colony I ventured there and saw them. I found many strange things there. When I told of what I found, the head elder, Abner was shocked and forbid anymore such ventures. The cryptic markings tell of a great quaking of the earth destroying the colony there. They also tell of other great colonies. Some were destroyed by fire from the sky. Some were destroyed by the clouds and others by great waters. The few people who lived after either formed colonies where ever they could or returned to the forest. It is said that civilized people were what caused the wind and earth and water to destroy the great colonies. After growing to manhood in the Ohio Valley Colony I think I understand why this is said.

My name is Zimm. I have only been a feral man for a few full seasons. This is plain in my language and because I can use the ancient markings to communicate. I have been tracking a feral female for some time now, the one named Vera. She left the civilized Ohio Valley Colony many seasons ago. She was not yet a woman when she left. She left for different reasons than I. I left to escape the squabbling of heartless elders over meaningless things while the fire wood was used up or the water urns ran dry. Vera left to escape the clutches of the head elder, Abner. He sought to possess her because she was smarter than most and because she was such a beautiful child. The elders of the colony had already begun vying for her attention with whatever favor their status could afford. But young Vera would have no part of their foul wants.

Several of the huntsmen were sent out in search of her when she left. The elders cried when it was discovered she was missing. Then they cried when they discovered some food rations were missing. Suddenly the loss of this beautiful young girl mattered less than a wicker basket of old potatoes. Several of the elders clamored for her blood. What sad specimens these elders of the colony are, drooling while waiting for this beautiful child to grow into a woman and when she steals some old potatoes to escape their insult they suddenly want her life. They would have her blood one way or another.

Vera was smart and every day she went out with the gathering party she would venture farther and farther from the colony's boundaries, always testing, always measuring. She constantly pestered me and other huntsmen for details of the hunt. It amused me to answer this young woman child's questions. I did not know she was learning all the while and would one day leave the colony. She had plotted well her path out of that civilized misery. Abner was right, she was smarter than most. It was said she would not last long without the protection of the colony. It was believed that she would starve or freeze to death or be carried off by rogue feral males. She has proven them all wrong. She thrives out here. She is spotted by huntsmen from the colony from time to time. On elder Abner's orders they try to catch her. They would easier catch a forest spirit. After she is spotted the colony speaks of it in hushed tones. The elders fear that others, tired of their pompous rule might go feral.

I am not yet as wild as Vera; I still, on occasion speak when I meet a colony hunting party. They always ask if I have seen her. I always lie and say no. They know I lie. They think that I, like every man of the colony want Vera for my own. They envy my skill in the forest for it keeps me close to her. They envy my steel tipped spear and my old time steel hand blades. They wonder how I have such tools. Vera has a steel tipped spear and old time steel hand blades. She got her old time steel hand blades the same place I got mine. When she left the colony she took a steel tipped spear from the supply hut along with the basket of old potatoes. Oh how the elders cried that one of the steel tipped spears had been stolen. She has long since discarded it and fashioned for herself a better one. I found the old spear embedded in the trunk of a hawthorn tree, I think she left it for me to find. She knows I follow her. There is nothing that happens in this valley that Vera doesn't know. Did I not know better I would think there was an entire colony of sinewy auburn women with pert breasts and steel tipped spears.

I am not her only follower. Several of the colony's woodsmen have been exiled for trying to find Vera without Abner's consent. If a huntsman or scout stays out longer than the elders think necessary he is beaten or exiled by order of Abner. Abner knows what he was doing... he was searching for Vera. I found one of Vera's campsites sometime back. There I found the body of a dead huntsman. He had a deep wound in his chest that went clear through. The wound was from the old time steel hand blade Vera has affixed to the end of her new spear. While examining the dead huntsman's wound I remembered how hard it was to pull her old spear from the hawthorn tree. Few men there are who can use a spear with such skill.

The huntsman is not the only man Vera has killed. She has also killed several rogue feral males. Living as she does, as I do, in the forest, encounters with rogue ferals happen from time to time and most often end in wounding or death. According to the elders of the Ohio Valley Colony all ferals are rogue. I have discovered this to be untrue. Most ferals avoid anyone they think to be civilized. I know several feral families. Knowing me to be feral they often wave or nod. Some even speak a few words. The elders always told us that a feral cannot speak, also untrue.

I have heard Vera speak since she went feral. Her voice sounds like spring water flowing over moss covered rocks. She was reciting poetry to herself as she bathed in a stream. This is the only time I have ever been near her that she did not know I was there. I want to believe she knew I was watching but I know the truth. My vantage point on a rocky ledge above her was too good. Vera guards closely her prize and will let no man close, civilized or feral. The elders taught her well that when a beautiful woman removes her cover in light of day, all men become feral. What would those pitiful elders at the colony give for what I have seen?

Her voice is as beautiful as her body. I could clearly hear the melody of her words. She still speaks well but her voice… there seems to be a slight cracking in her throat as if she is about to cry. When I heard it I felt as if I might cry. I have noticed as time passes my voice weakens if I fail to use it so I speak often to myself, except when on the hunt. The elders tell me I talked too much as a child. They also told me I asked too many questions. I was being taught to use the ancient cryptic markings for communication until I made the mistake of asking about the stones with the markings. I was beaten and told to never visit the place with the marked stones again.

I have long since discovered the mystery of the stones with markings, though I have yet to discovered why the elders so objected to me reading the markings. I think they fear it will somehow threaten their status. Anything that will threaten an elder's status is strictly forbidden. The elders wield their status like a steel tipped spear, commanding which of the people will fetch the water, who will gather fire wood, who will get a potato.

Vera was once put before the elders for reading the stones with the markings. She was not beaten because Abner already longed for her. Vera could have been an elder had she wanted, though few women are. Everyone in the colony knew that when Vera became a woman she would have great status because of her wisdom as a youth, even more because she was so pleasing to the eye. She wanted none of that and was good at concealing her feelings for the elders. Abner could not conceal his want for Vera nor could I conceal my disdain for Abner. After Abner became leader, it was ruled that the elders would choose the people's duties and not all members would be taught the ancient cryptic markings for communication. Only because I understood the ancient markings did I make the discoveries in the place called Cleveland that made me the greatest hunter of the Ohio Valley. Before

Abner became head elder what I found there would have been celebrated by the people.

I kept my discoveries to myself and used what I knew for the benefit of the colony. Between the times of my findings in the place called Cleveland and several full seasons ago something within the hearts of the people changed. Not many of the young men were taught to hunt and a heaviness set upon the colony. As time passed the young men no longer wanted to learn to hunt. Bringing back enough meat for the colony became difficult, even for me and some people went without.

One day as I sat exhausted, after a long, unsuccessful hunt I remembered an incident from my youth. I had used an expression the elders say was from the old days, long before the time of the Ohio Valley Colony. I thought the expression; "Ram it" must surely refer to a spear thrust. When I was overheard saying this aloud to myself an elder quickly took me aside and explained the meaning, telling me to never utter those words aloud to anyone or I would be exiled from the colony. I have said those words to myself many times since then. I think Vera said these words to herself early in her life.

I now approach a campsite I know to be Vera's. I know this because several days ago I found her foot prints on this trail. It leads to the open valley where she hunts. When at times I find her campsite it is only after she has abandoned it. Vera has learned well the ways of the forest and knows a good campsite must have one trail that leads to hunting grounds and several hidden trails leading to escape. As I stealth my way slowly down the trail to her campsite I notice movement and the next moment I am frozen in wonder. There, only thirty paces away she stands. Her hazel eyes looking at me feel like a stab in my heart. She stands erect but leans slightly on her spear. I know at once she does not fear me or she would not let herself be seen. Because of the warm time in the valley she is naked but for a buck skin belt and sheath. I notice in the sheath is one of the old time steel hand blades like mine. I feel a kindling in my inner most being. Her skin is tanned and glistened with sweat, the sinew of her arms and legs have the look of cypress bark. Her breasts are pointed and firm and stand out proudly. I see a drop of sweat running down between them and I taste salt in my mouth. Her eyes go from mine slowly to my sheath and she notices my old time steel hand blade and approval shows on her face. Now her eyes move to my loin skin and for a moment she looks at me as if I might be an elder, but only for a moment before her expression and her stance soften and I hear that slight cracking of her voice.

"You once hunted for the Ohio Valley Colony. Are you not the one called Zimm? When I was young, it was you who would answer my questions about the hunt."

I nod yes, unable to speak. She takes a few more steps towards me letting the shaft of her spear slide through her fingers to drag behind her. Her eyes again drop to my loin skin and I feel a fire growing beneath it. She quickly looks up to meet my eyes.

"Why do you not speak now, you speak when in the forest. The only time you do not speak is when you hunt."

"You know much about my ways young woman. You speak very little; speak again for your voice is a pleasing sound."

"Did you not hear me speak not long ago as I bathed in the stream? You were on a rocky ledge above me."

My breath is taken by her words. I now know I am not the slyest creature in the forest as I believed I was. I wonder if she is a forest spirit for she has watched me many times and I knew not that she was near. The thought of this beautiful creature nearby without my knowledge forces me to smile. With her free hand she pushes her tangled auburn hair back from her eyes and steps closer, a smile growing on her face and I feel warmth inside my being. Her look intensifies and she asked,

"This memory pleases you as well?"

She searches my face as one might search the forest floor for signs of game. As I gaze into her eyes I feel a yearning growing in my heart. We are robbed of this moment by a slight crackle in a thicket by the trail. Deep inside, I curse this intrusion but only for an instant. At the same moment I touch my hand blade I see Vera change her grip on the shaft of her spear. Without breaking eye contact we listen to the forest. As we listen her eyes become so deep they threatened to suffocate me. I feel she can read my thoughts and all the forest knows of the surging in my heart. In an instant there is a crashing of something through the thicket beside the trail and I see Vera's relaxed body turn to sinew as she leans away from her spear pulling it into a mighty thrust as easily as one would toss a dried corn stalk. I hear the sound of wind as it flies several paces past me, disappearing into the thicket over the head of a charging hunting Ker. In a flash my blade is out and I give the snarling Ker my forearm as it springs from the forest floor. The instant before its jaws snap shut, I plunge my blade to the hilt in the Ker's neck and twist it as the animal's momentum takes me to the ground.

I am up in a moment, my hand blade ready. Vera has her hand blade out, alert for any sound. We stand listening for several moments before our eyes again meet.

I look her up and down. Her body of sinew is still tight as she grips her hand blade, standing ready, her legs parted and I am reminded of a deer about to take flight. Her body is wet with sweat and her breasts glisten; the pale brown nipples in longing. She breaks eye contact and her eyes move to my forearm. I am aware of the wound from the bite of the Ker but feel no pain, only aware of the fire beneath my lion skin and in my chest. I take in her beauty and my eyes stop at the auburn mound that is just below the tie of her buck skin belt. I notice small beads of sweat clinging to the fine blond hair of her inner thigh.

Then I look into her eyes to see what I believe to be a fire as hot as my own. Now we hear another sound from the thicket, that of a struggle for life. Vera moves close to my side and her touch burns as she takes my arm. I part the briers to see a huntsman, half sitting; half slumped with Vera's spear penning him to the trunk of a large sycamore tree. He clings to the shaft as he struggled to support his weight. I recognized this huntsman; he is from the Ohio Valley Colony. Vera's spear has hit him low and penetrated cleanly. I grab the huntsman by his hair and pull his face to mine. He winces in pain and his eyes are full of terror.

"You are from the colony." The man struggles in pain to answer.

"Yes ... I am Arcon, elder Abner sent me. I lead a hunting party in search of the woman Vera ... and the rogue called Zimm."

"And why does Abner seek this Vera?"

"The colony is in need, Abner offers her eldership."

I reaffirm my grip in his tangled hair and pull him closer. "And this rogue you speak of?"

"Abner has ordered his death."

At his words I feel Vera's body tighten. I pull from her and grasp the spear's shaft with both hands and madly yank it, freeing Arcon from the tree. He cries out as he falls to the ground gasping. I toss Vera's spear aside and turn to her. We find each other's eyes and stand motionless, listening to the forest until we are sure we are alone. Then our mouths meet with such want we ignore the bruising of our lips between our teeth. When I am sure I have committed her taste to memory for life I release her. She holds my face in her hands and looks to Arcon as his dying breath escapes him. Clinging to my face she looks back into my eyes and speaks.

"Had Arcon lived I would have him tell Abner that Vera does not belong in the colony, but here, in the forest, with Zimm."

Now she takes my hand and leads me towards her campsite.

The Two Faces of Beauty

The Kiamichi River is one of eight rivers that flow from Pine Mountain in Arkansas. On a map this collection of streams looks like the legs of a spider, the Kiamichi being the western most leg. In life, it looks like heaven and the Kiamichi River and the country it runs through is one of the most beautiful works of nature you will ever see.

It meanders through the rocky, piney woods of Arkansas to the Eastern border of Oklahoma, and then starts turning south through the Kiamichi Mountains where it eventually meets the Red River on the Texas/ Oklahoma State line. Not far from there is where this adventure took place.

The Kiamichi is a slow, peaceful, shoal filled ribbon that could easily run through the Garden of Eden. Hardly passing for a river most of the time, simply add water and it can become hell. This was the case on Thanksgiving Day of 1985. The Kiamichi was higher than any of the residents of Antlers Oklahoma had ever seen it. Officially speaking it was higher than it had been in over fifty years. That day it bore no resemblance to the blue ribbon that gently flowed through the Garden of Eden.

Remembering it I get cold chills down my back, realizing that at the time I saw no inherent danger. Of course I had only been bitten by the "River Ratting" bug a short time earlier. The fact that I write this must prove that God's guardian angels watched over me, because River Ratting, that is, the exploration of an unknown river by isolated free floating isn't something that you would one day say, "Oh, that looks fun, I can do that." All facts and logic aside, that was exactly what I had done. And so there I stood at the banks of a rushing torrent of water that only two weeks before was a peaceful blue ribbon.

The Kiamichi River trip was only about the second or third really serious river trip I had organized and launched entirely on my own. Of all the river accidents I have suffered, this one was not only the worst but the most preventable. There are those cold chills again ... As any good river rat will tell you; every river has its own personality, just like a woman. And just like a woman, her own beauty, her own pleasures, her own desires. Also, not unlike a woman, her own dangers unique to her and as with any river, just add or take away water and her personality changes. Some grow more loving, some become wicked, and some change for the better or worse depending upon the topographical layout of the land it courses through. That is one of the mysteries of a river, especially an undammed river, because a thunder storm hundreds of miles away can change your river ratting experience without you even knowing it is raining.

We were dropped off that fateful day at the intersection of the Kiamichi River and Highway 271, just north of Antlers, Oklahoma, at about 8:00 AM on a beautiful, 40 degree, overcast day. Our plans were to free float from this intersection to Rattan Landing some thirty miles away, as the crow flies. One lesson I learned well that day, a crow flying has very little to do with the flowing of a river. Depending on the circumstances, thirty miles can be a couple hours, a couple days, or never. We would find out just how far thirty miles could be.

We had fair equipment, two Sevelor six hundred and fifty pound capacity inflatable rafts tethered together so we each had an ore to work, I in the raft on the left, Steve on the right. Inflatable rafts can be a pain in the ass. Every form of boating has advantages and disadvantages. Ours displayed the best and worst of its type of boat that day, and in fact, saved our lives.

It was somewhat difficult launching, what with water flowing at 12 to 15 miles per hour through the tops of fifty foot tall trees. The fact that this usually twenty to thirty yard wide stream was now over one hundred yards wide in places didn't seem to faze us in the least. I say us, I didn't care and my partner and brother-in-law, Steve didn't know any better. Two weeks before we had been there and had plotted a trek to the river's bank some thirty yards away and down. Now there was no trekking thirty yards down a stone strewn path to the water. This would be much easier, we thought. Actually it wasn't that hard and I made no connection between the difficulties of putting into this raging torrent and getting out of it. We managed to control the rafts while loading them, getting in and getting comfortable. We were able to let ourselves out into the swift current, at which time we released the tie line and suddenly… we had wind in our faces.

While I can look back now and shiver at how fast we were going, all I felt at the time was exhilaration. I do remember the look on Steve's face. I had been on at least a couple fast rivers before, but nothing like this. It was not white water, but flood water. When we got the boats righted and Steve realized we did have some control over our direction, his expression became more relaxed. I popped the top on a beer, fired up a joint and presto, instant fun. One of the sad aspects of this story is that the fun didn't last long, not long at all. I had just finished my joint and my beer, the only ones I would have that day, and ahead was a monstrous fork in the river. What was this, the Kiamichi River didn't fork… Oh yes it did, and no time to question why, the only question was, left branch-right branch?

As we had put in on the southern bank we needed the right branch. For some reason Steve questioned this and wanted to at least get close enough to the fork to look down the left branch. For no other reason than out of respect for my best friend and brother-in-law we maintained a rather too-much center of the river position. Alas, it was already too late. Suddenly we were only fifty or sixty yards from the fork, except now reality came sharply into focus as we saw what this fork really looked like, a tremendous breastwork of hundred year old tree trunks from up state. Hell, some of them were from out of state. Suddenly, for the first time I felt something of what might be called apprehension.

Actually, I was momentarily paralyzed with fear, and as calmly as I could say it I told Steve we needed to make for the right hand fork of the river for all we were worth. I began rowing like a mad man, which only put us in a spin because Steve seemed to not be responding. Now suddenly we were only a matter of yards from the first logs and Steve began to row hard. It was too, too late. I saw there was no way to avoid hitting the log jam and so had to make stuff up as I went along. All I could say was, "Do what I do, Steve!" Just as we hit the first log I leaned forward on my ore. Like some desperate jouster I found anchor on the log and it forced us into a counter-clockwise spin. Steve instinctively did what I had just done and our counter-clockwise spin continued rolling us along the right hand side of the log jam and hopefully back into the right hand fork of the river. Our desperate spin continued and again it was my turn… No place to put my ore.

I tried but it slipped between two tree trunks. Our rafts were tethered together, mine on the left, Steve's on the right, and we hit the log jam fairly head on and our counter-clock wise spin continued enough that Steve's raft washed up partially on the log jam. My raft partially swamped with many gallons of 40 degree water.

There we were with Steve's raft partially up on a three foot diameter tree trunk and my raft out in the current moving up and down with the undulation of the river. When we hit the log jam the level of the river was up and nothing drastic happened, other than my raft swamping with water. About every twenty or thirty seconds the undulation would cause the level of the river to drop or raise about a foot. Because Steve's raft was up on the logs, the first drop we experienced only further flooded my raft. Suddenly I realized I had until the next drop in the level of the river to do something. Separate the rafts, the only option, an impossible one, but I had to try. As I fumbled with the ties the water level began to drop until the water began to flood my raft with no place to go. My raft, its contents and I were swept under the log jam. Sometime between this last swamping of my raft and the time I was out of the water enough to see light and to breathe again, I had one of those experiences they speak of where the entire sum of your life passes before you. I won't try to describe this, for it is surely one of those experiences that defy description and will only divert from this story long enough to say that the experience so impressed me that it stood out from all else that was happening.

Fortunately the same rush of water that had doomed me pushed Steve's raft up firmly on the log jam or it and he would have followed me under. I remember total darkness for only a moment then climbing up on the log jam several yards from Steve and our distressed rafts. My raft was wrapped under a large tree trunk, its main air compartment hopelessly ruptured, and pinned by the swift current. As I climbed back over an obstacle course of ever shifting logs I tried to form a plan of action in my mind. We were able to untie the damaged raft and work it up from under the log jam. Damaged as it was it aided our efforts to return to civilization. We were able to get both rafts up on the log jam and out of the current.

From the outer edge of the log jam, where water meets wood, to the shore, was less than forty yards. So close, yet so far. As we sat precariously on the log jam the water rushed violently through the logs and every so often logs in the log jam would shift as the force of the river rearranged them according to its liking. As the river rearranged the logs, we rearranged the rafts, strapping all the equipment that wasn't lost into the damaged raft. To do this we were forced to put Steve's raft over the first log subjecting it to the force of the current that ran through the log jam. We attached a tie line to a stubbed off limb of a log and Steve clung to it holding the raft in place while I very carefully made my way to Steve's raft across the shifting logs. Finally, with me in Steve's raft and thinking we were ready, Steve let loose the tie line and we rushed forward five or six yards to the next set of logs. Carefully we coaxed our rafts over the logs to the next short opening of rushing water and repeated the process, slamming into the next set of logs. All the while the entire mass of logs writhed and moaned as the current continued to subject them to nature's unimaginable force.

The closer we got to the shore, the more tightly the logs were packed and the less current that surged through them. Finally we drug our rafts off the last logs and onto solid ground, where we both collapsed from total exhaustion. We were off that dammed log jam!

Now we were on a hopelessly isolated V in the middle of a hundred yard wide river we had just fought so hard to get off of. No matter, we were off the log jam. Probably an hour passed before we caught our breath and was up, doing an equipment inventory and damage assessment. Equipment: much less than we started with. Damage: my raft had a ruptured main compartment. The floor and side compartments still held air. Steve's raft was basically still intact, except for one small thing... a slow leak in the main compartment. We looked high and low but could not determine where the leak was. Again, it was decision time. Not knowing if the leak was a puncture or a seam failure was a vexing question. You see the former, no big deal, you lose a little air, and the raft gets soft. Now the latter, a seam failure, is a different story altogether. When a seam failure is subjected to further stress it can become a real problem very quickly.

After further inspection we decided, somewhat expediently, to treat the leak as a puncture. We really didn't have much choice as our options were few indeed. Again we prepared to put back in with intentions of crossing the river and determining how far we were from civilization. Hopefully not too far at this point. I looked out across the water at the tops of the nearly submerged trees I had scoffed at when we launched feeling as if they now scoffed at me. Suddenly the difficulties facing us getting off this river became painfully clear to me. The fear I felt considering getting back on this raging torrent in two damaged rafts was of a different nature than the fear I had just experienced. I had plenty of time to ponder this because it took some time before we found a place to even try to put back in. We found a small inlet where the current was not overpowering and were able to begin again.

In a moment we had the wind in our face, clipping along headed for the Southern bank. We crossed the river quickly but as we tried again and again to disembark, the miles passed. Finally we came upon a large inlet with no current and got off the river. We breathed a long breath of relief for we were entirely winded. As we rested Steve mentioned a strange feeling he had had when we first hit the log jam and I was swept under. He rather stoically commented, "You were gone." As we spoke I realized this was the first conversation we had had not directly related to our survival. I told Steve about my experience with my life passing before me and what a profound experience it was.

As rested as possible we deflated both rafts and fashioned a sled of sorts and began a southerly trek in hopes of finding a road. What time was it? Steve was the only one with a watch and it was not functioning. We needed no watch to know it was late in the day. As the sun fell the ground became soggy as we came upon some river backwater that stretched as far as the eye could see. Had it been light enough to see I am sure our faces would have expressed our feelings at the discovery of this backwater. We tried slogging but soon discovered the water was too deep. With fatigued resign we unloaded the rafts and began the arduous task of inflating them without the benefit of a pump, which was long gone. By the time we found solid ground again our one remaining flashlight was near drained. Repeating our previous routine of converting from river rats to sled dogs we continued our journey.

One of the beautiful things about being that far out in the woods at night is the stars. Several times we were so awe struck by the diamond dust above us we would stop and just look and expressed profound gratitude to the heavens for what we were experiencing. You never know what you have lost until you lose it and what we were seeing was something lost to city dwellers.

As we continued to trudge, our legs began to feel the strain and we noticed that several degrees above what should be the horizon there were no stars. We shined our faded flashlight beam forward but could determine nothing. Had we been able to see each other's faces I'm sure we would have had expressions similar to the ones we wore when we first came upon the river backwater. We pushed on and it wasn't long and the mystery of the starless horizon was solved, we had reached the foot of a steep incline. So our starless horizon was a sharp rise in elevation. After another hour we realized it was not a sharp rise in elevation, but a drastic one. Not only were we struggling up a 45 degree, rock strewn, tree covered slope, but now our only flashlight was completely dead.

It took over two hours to climb to level ground. When we got there we could see lights in the distance, the few late night lights of Antlers Oklahoma. We walked through a cow pasture to a black top road, stashed our supplies and continued our journey wondering how much longer our legs would support us. It was well after mid-night when we woke everyone up, back much earlier than we were expected. We drove back and retrieved our remaining supplies.

I have had some very long days in my life; this was one of the longest. Steve and I spoke of this day several times, but it was clear to me that Steve's curiosity about the river had been well satisfied. I knew he wanted no more "isolated free floating" of unexplored rivers. For me ... it only made me more fanatical about River Ratting. I have been on many rivers since and I am, in fact planning my next trip as I write this. Please wish me luck.

Final Reflections of Virgil Woolf

I wonder if this table will collapse under the weight of
the clutter it supports. A vast field of empty prescription
bottles, soda cans, old mail and the detritus of a life sadly
lived. Dear old Mrs. Wiggins, I know the conditions I
live under drive her crazy. Driven her to drink she says.
"Virgil, how can you live like this?" I hear it all the time.
Or, "Virgil, when are you going to do all those dishes?"
And the old stand-by, "Virgil, you've had that same shirt
on for a week." Still, she is more patient with my slobbish
ass than my other landladies were. "Virgil, this apartment
sure is all crapped up, you'll draw roaches." She worries
about the old pizza boxes. I wonder what her reaction
will be when she finds me. I wonder if her heart will give
out when she finds my bloated, swollen carcass covered
in blow flies. I bet the carbon monoxide will run all my
roaches upstairs. That would be real poetic justice. Poetic
justice . . . that is what destroyed me. Poetry. Of course
the novel didn't help either. Oh Well it will all soon be
behind me. This is if Hershel is correct on what he says.
But if Hershel knows so much why is he still alive? He
assures me that carbon monoxide is painless. Says the only
thing, it will turn my skin bright red. Who cares, I won't
be here to see it. So I will sit here with my whisky bottle

and my valium and wait for death to come. The car seems to be idling a little rough. Oh well, if it dies I'll restart it . . . or use the lawn mower. That's the good thing about living in a garage apartment that is an actual garage. Arm chair comfort while you gas yourself.

Ah company . . . Solenopsis invecta, is that you? Ah yes, Solenopsis wrestling with a pizza crumb. Go, take all the crumbs you like, it will leave less for poor old Mrs. Wiggins to clean up after I'm . . . well, gone. Brought some friends with you, eh? Greedy little shits. I guess you ants must make a living, too. So how is the pizza crumb business? Great as long as you have burnt out writers to fling empty pizza boxes in all directions, huh? But, when I'm gone, what will you do then? What will your mighty queen ant say to you then? Is it she that tells you where to go, what to carry? She sits on her ass giving orders. I bet you don't even get any of the crumb, do you? You wrestle a crumb weighing hundreds of times your own weight, and for what? You're a communist, nothing more. Nothing but a greedy little commie. Your little caravan looks like the Ho Chi Min Trail. Yes, that's it, little communist on the Pizza Crumb Trail. Stumbling blindly along with your prize. All to be given to your great leader back at the colony. Hershel says ants will conquer the world someday. He said that about the communist, too. Hershel, what does he know? Tried to overdose on Benadryl. What a lame bastard my best friend is. Tells me I drink too much. At least I drink good whisky, not that damn gin he and old Mrs. Wiggins drink. He thinks drinking gin is fashionable, en vogue, trendy. Ever since he read that Norton's Anthology of British Literature he thinks he is Robert Lewis Stevenson. Thinks drinking gin will make him a better writer.

Feels like my eyes are burning a little. Maybe Hershel was right for once. Maybe the pollution control gizmos won't filter out all the carbon monoxide. I wonder if the carbon monoxide will kill the ants. This endless trail of six-legged little communists who now hoard all my excess pizza crumbs. Does the fumes burn their eyes as well? What do the ants think about as they struggle with their loads? Do they hope ol' Queeny will be pleased? What is it like to be an ant? Were an ant a writer, what would he write about? "The Life and Times on the Pizza Crumb Trail." And look here, a straggler, a maverick, one single ant not in line. So what is your story, Nomad? What caused you to break away from the group? Don't you know, if news of your wandering gets back to ol' Queeny, she will rain down punishment on you? It's always the same. Those who break away. Those who think differently. "Gulp . . ." Ah, good whisky. About the only thing I will miss on the other side. Gad Zooks, the Nomad has found something! Cucaracha! And it's on! A death struggle with a juvenile cucaracha! Mandibles dig in deep, legs braced . . . ah, the stinger stabs. Look at that little bugger fight to no avail. What pain that formic acid must cause. He struggles . . . struggles . . . the struggle is at last over. Well, Nomad, are you pleased with yourself? Now some mother roach weeps for her lost child. You will carry your quarry back and the Queen will be pleased. All these other . . . ants brought back pizza crumbs, but no, you brought back fresh meat. Now you can look down your nose at your fellows. Just like my friend Hershel.

Smug bastard. With the proceeds from his new book he can now afford to drink himself to death in style. Just like ol' Jack Kerouac did. My eyes are really burning and I'm dizzy. I guess Hershel was right about carbon monoxide. I feel faint. One more drink . . . "gulp". Upon reflection, I don't want Hershel to be right. I'm not ready to check out. I feel faint. I'll abandon this suicide nonsense for now. I'll switch the motor off and go to bed. I'll sleep this off and return to my writing. But first I'll just lay my head down a moment . . .

Incident at Zaragoza

Reconnaissance confirmed that about one hundred Lucha Dangelaro insurgents were only a short distance from San Rabio, a peaceful village fifteen kilometers south of the Zaragoza River in Southern Panama. Though lightly armed they were a threat to the village. They advanced down the Via Paloma Road – a decaying paved road that reached to within a few kilometers of the bridge at Delgato. One battered American Dodge truck was reported to have a long tube-like piece of equipment mounted on the bed. Franco suspected a Soviet 122mm rocket launcher – a nasty concern that can "bring big smoke." To delay their advance, a few clever fellows were dispatched to destroy the bridge at Delgato that spanned the turbulent Zaragoza River.

How I became a party to this rag-tag group of would-be saviors, led by a Panamanian CIA operative, was sheer coincidence. As a writer and avid river exploration freak, I was given a rare opportunity to survey a short uncharted stretch of the legendary Zaragoza River in Southern Panama. This was set up by my publisher who had a friend in government, who had a friend at the Panamanian Embassy, who had a friend, who had a friend. I lost track of who did what. All the while I kept hearing hushed mention of the, Lucha Dangelaro, a drug gang committing robberies and violence in the name of Marx in southern Panama around the Zaragoza River. Lately it seems their numbers had increased, as well as their crimes. Yet when I officially requested information – any Embassy warning – no one would even acknowledge there was such a group. If the Embassy didn't acknowledge these thugs, there must not be much to them.

I was more worried about the Bushmasters that infested the jungles there. Ah, the Bushmaster: Lachesis Muta, an ornery bastard attaining lengths of over twelve feet. Lachesis has the second longest fangs in the snake world – over two inches. A bite in the field is certain death and even with anti-venom a victim still has less than a fifty-fifty chance of survival, and then will suffer severe heart or nerve damage. The Lucha Dangelaro was way down on my list of worries.

When the Panamanian River Society (P. R. S.) called and offered to sponsor my expedition, I forgot all about the Lucha Dangelaro and their reptilian counterpart. My publisher would get a submission to read, the P. R. S. would get a report, and I would get to do what I love: float a new river, and then write about it.

The Zaragoza River is unique among rivers. Located in the south of Panama, it is sustained by underground aqueducts that give varying amounts of water. It only rages when it rains enough to overflow the Golo Basin, up high in the hills. This can happen at any given hour and when it does, the Zaragoza flows in two directions, bisecting the Isthmus of Panama – west to the Golfo de Panama, east to the Caribbean Sea. For now it was calm . . . for the Zaragoza River.

I would put in (launch) at San Rabio, a small village, and with a combination of free-floating and rowing, float west to the bridge at Delgato. I would take a few days, a week, however long I wanted. That is the beauty of "isolated free floating"; all you need is a launch point, a pick-up point and a little knowledge of what lies between the two. A few tattered topographical maps furnished by the P. R. S. and interviews with some of the locals in San Rabio would suffice. The bridge at Delgato was a simple, but stout heavy wooden frame supported by four twelve-inch diameter poles. It spanned the two banks – approximately thirty-five feet – and stood over twenty feet above the swift current. The only problem was the bridge was actually a couple kilometers from the village. But, as time was not pressing I would cut a trail to the river. This would be easy enough because a semblance of a trail ran to within a short distance of the Via Paloma Road that led to the bridge. It took much longer than I had imagined.

When I first reached the American Embassy, I met a fellow I would see again, Franco Valderman. I first noticed him talking to an American Marine Lieutenant. Then I saw him here and there as I prepared for my expedition. He seemed to get around a lot. I wondered about his presence until I managed to "accidentally" catch him following me as I worked on the trail I would use to return from the river. He laughed when he realized I had managed to disappear, and then come up behind him. I could have laughed too, had he not brandished a Sig Sauer P-226 – 9mm pistol with blinding speed. It was this incident that broke the ice. We became friends and Franco wasn't too surprised when I suggested that his Sig 9mm was "issued." But, it wasn't just the fifteen hundred dollar pistol that made me suspicious. Franco's neck and forearms – they hinted at a thousand fingertip push-ups a day. People don't maintain olympic – level fitness to be tour guides. Of course he never admitted to anything. But surely he was some elite military hybrid. He did give me some specific information about the Lucha Dangelaro, "meaner than 'Matas Caballo." This is Spanish for "kill a horse" a reference to the potency of the Bushmaster's venom.

Franco knew of the P. R. S. sponsorship of my expedition. He finally confessed to me that keeping me from harm's way was an unofficial assignment.

"So you are agency . . . ?" Franco smiled, but made no reply. It was through Franco that I obtained a Ruger MK-II .22 cal pistol, a couple of extra magazines and one hundred rounds of old Winchester High-Speed ammunitions – just a security measure.

I had camped at the bridge at Delgato the night after finishing the trail. I was exhausted. I had crossed the bridge after dawn to discover a stunning view from a cliff that overlooked the Via Paloma road's approach from the north. Amazing, of all the jungle you could see for miles. I took several shots with my Canon 3100. I had just crossed back over when I heard the sound of movement on the trail. I retrieved the Ruger MK-II from my pack and took cover behind a giant Philodendron. Minutes later I heard Franco call out, "River Rat, its Valderman…"

I was surprised and curious. Franco and two others stepped into my campsite. All dressed in full woodland camos, all armed, and an air of urgency about them. Franco spoke in hurried Spanish so I only caught bits and pieces of what he said – something about avoiding any direct contact with the Lucha Dangelaro. When he caught me staring at what I recognized as C-4 general-purpose explosive and #2 radio wire, he introduced me.

"This is Eduardo, my demo-man. We don't have much time." He quickly explained to me that my river trip was postponed. When he ordered another fellow to reconnoiter the North bank, I found myself speaking; "I already have, there is this killer view..." Franco showed a faint glint of a smile. I felt he read my mind thinking; this was bound to be more fun that floating the river.

"Say River Rat, no American agencies are officially operating south of the Panama Canal . . ." There was a certain gravity in his words. I waved him off.

"I'm not agency; I'm a rafter, besides ya'll are in a hurry." He nodded to another man he had just introduced as Bobby, who I recognized as the Marine Lieutenant, at the embassy.

"Lieutenant Norton – go with the good American." When we reached the cliff movement was clear in the valley below. Lieutenant Norton whispered to me, "Pinchy Muta".

I saw what he was referring to. A fuming old Dodge pick-up with a large recoilless rifle mounted on the bed.

"Simple bandits?" I asked. We hurried back to give warning. As we crossed the bridge Franco motioned for us to take cover quickly. As I looked back, my heart pounding in my ears, I saw several insurgents emerge from the woods on the North bank. All armed with Soviet AK-47's and all looking in our direction. I noticed Eduardo had connected the radio wire to a standard M-3 detonation generator. All eyes were transfixed as two insurgents stepped onto the bridge. I caught Franco's look as if to say, "Oh well". Suddenly one of the insurgents yelled out,

"Alambre Alambre". Franco quickly but calmly ordered,

"Blow it," Eduardo replied,

"Fuego en el pozo", and twisted the crank on the detonator. A bright orange flame enveloped the bridge momentarily. The bank shook violently and the air was suddenly filled with thick, black caustic tasting smoke. Bits of wood and splinters of all sizes rained down. As the reverberations of the explosion died out we became aware of the rattle of small arms fire coming from the North bank. We were well on our way, but the whiz of 7.62 rounds followed us for some time. We returned to San Rabio believing the village was safe, at least temporarily. Franco never mentioned any repercussions from the death of the two insurgents on the bridge.

Note: It is not the policy of the American government to conduct covert operations on foreign soil. Any mention of American agencies or US military materiel, equipment, operations, or locations of such operations, are, of course fictionalized.

Silent Plains

Political intrigue in our great country has a long and colorful history and has taken many forms. The old west is no exception and is replete with examples. One such case being that of General George Armstrong Custer and his demise at the Battle of the Little Bighorn, and at first glance it seems an open and shut case. The most commonly known version of this "wild west" story being that an overly confident Custer was simply overwhelmed by the combined forces of the Lakota Cheyenne, Sioux and Arapaho warriors. However if one researches this subject they are soon faced with many unanswered questions.

Conspiracy theories have abounded through the years. Of course, only since the age of mass media, investigative journalism and reporters who doggedly pursue any lead, has any theory caused much controversy. Deep inquiry of these controversies often raises as many questions as they answer. The nature of an investigation – if not impeded by outside influences – is final closure. Enough facts are finally discovered to give a general description of how an act was carried out and a possible motive. When any investigation or inquiry raises more questions than it answers, a conspiracy can be reasonably inferred.

Seldom is any controversial act carried out without leaving trace evidence. The same is true of the Battle of the Little Big Horn and you soon realize it shares many unsettling features with more modern conspiracy theories.

The nature of intrigue is that it obscures facts leaving unanswered questions that must never be answered if the cover up is to remain intact. So let us examine the "facts" as best we can from our chronological proximity.

George A. Custer graduated from West Point at the bottom of his class in 1861. There he earned excessive demerits and stayed close to expulsion the entire four years he attended. Custer distinguished himself in the Civil War and was the youngest man to ever attain generalship and second youngest general at the war's end. Custer's recklessness earned him a reputation for bravery. It also earned him the scorn of many who blamed his foolhardiness for high losses among his men.

But it is during the Indian wars that troubling questions begin to accumulate. In 1876, Hiester Clyman, Chairman of the House Committee on Military Expenditures, conducted an investigation into the dealings of Secretary William W. Belknap and George Custer was a key witness. All who took part in these proceedings acknowledge that Custer's testimony was hearsay. Despite this unusual aspect, it seems that Custer's testimony was damning. Not just against Belknap, but his testimony also implicated Orville Grant, the brother of President Grant.

Grant had Custer relieved of command and arrested. A short time later Custer was reinstated as a Lt. Colonel and Commander of the 7th Cavalry. On May 17th, 1876, the 7th Cavalry totaling eleven hundred men left Fort Lincoln headed for an appointment with fate.

Here the questions veer sharply into the unanswerable. First, over three quarters of the 7th Cavalry did not even take part in the Battle of the Little Big Horn. Various (somewhat dubious) ad hoc explanations for this exist. None make much sense. One is that Major Benteen's flanking maneuver was stopped by an attack at the Little Bighorn River. Modern forensic investigative methods show no such attack took place.

Another is that Captain Reno got lost. This is a bit hard to accept in view of the fact that not only was this all taking place in the "plains" but Captain Reno also had a half dozen Indian scouts who called these plains their home.

But there are even more troubling questions for which there are no answers at all: where did the over five-hundred repeating rifles used by the hostile tribes come from? In fact, modern forensic investigation reveals that over forty different types of firearms using self-contained ammunition was used against Custer and the 7th Cavalry. The question posed by these rifles and the thousands of rounds of ammunition these hostile, non-treaty warriors possessed is one for which there is no reasonable explanation; and the odor of something amiss increases as we examine the history of these rifles.

Among the repeating rifles used against Custer's 7th Cavalry were two hundred Henry rifles, two hundred Winchester model 1866's and over one hundred Spencer repeating rifles. First, the Henry rifle which was the creation of Ben Tyler Henry in 1860 and an actual forerunner to today's assault rifle. It held up to sixteen rounds of .44 Remington rim fire. The 200 grain round nose bullet exited the muzzle at about 1100 feet per second. It was easily accurate enough to hit a human sized target at 200 yards, and with a little practice, the shooter could discharge all sixteen rounds in a very short time. While the Henry rifle saw some action in the War Between the States, its cost was prohibitive. At $52.50 each, it was worth several months pay for the average man. Approximately 14,000 Henry rifles were produced before B. T. Henry went broke and sold his company to Oliver Winchester. Winchester produced an improved version in 1866. Ordinance Department records show that the U. S. Government purchased 1,731. The serial numbers are in a narrow range from 3,000 to 4,200, some 531 not listed. The National Archives show that 1,544 Henry rifles were purchased, a discrepancy of about two hundred rifles. There is also an unexplained overlapping of serial numbers with the last Henry rifles produced and the first Winchester 1866 models. Ordinance records in the Washington, D. C. Archive's list the serial numbers ranging from 1392 to 3956, noted on a purchase made December 30, 1863. There are no existing records on the Winchester rifles with overlapping serial numbers. I suspect their identification would shed light on the subject. There are several dozen Henry rifles in private collections bearing the suspect serial numbers, proving they were among the ones purchased by the U. S. government. Most of these rifles can be traced back to purchases made at Bureau of Indian Affairs auctions.

We also know the Bureau of Indian Affairs had full time scouts tracking the hostile, non-treaty tribes. Much of the time these scouts did not know the location of the tribes. The argument that "gun runners" furnished the-over five hundred- repeating rifles is stretched beyond believability in view of this and other facts. Earlier there was money to be made by selling guns and whisky to the

Indians. The fungible commodity used by the hostile tribes was gold and animal furs. By the 1870's the fur trade had dropped off sharply and the Indians were even more likely than whites to mistake iron pyrite (fool's gold) for the real thing. Aside from the fact that any kind of unauthorized trading with hostile non-treaty tribes was a hanging offense, it is difficult to believe that many freelance traders had the resources to range over thousands of square miles with dozens of wagons seeking to trade with Indians that professional trackers often could not find.

The Bureau of Indian Affairs had, without doubt, the best scouts and the most uninterrupted communication with the non-treaty tribes. This fact coupled with the bewildering question of how the most technologically advanced weapon of the day found its way into the hands of the hostile, non-treaty warriors in such numbers is indeed unsettling.

Another suspicious aspect of this story is that George Custer was doing research on the Arapaho, Sioux and Lakota Cheyenne tribes and requesting reports relating to Indian agents and certain possible conflicts of interest. Ironically these same tribes would annihilate George Armstrong Custer and two hundred seventy seven men on July 25, 1876.

History has faithfully recorded the American people's reaction to the Battle of the Little Big Horn. The sympathy that had been mounting for the Plains Indians was swept away by a national cry for revenge. Yet the actions of Major Marcus Reno and Captain Fredrick Benteen – the two commanders who abandoned Custer at the critical moment – were never questioned. Perhaps if this and other questions had been asked the prevailing story of this incident would be different. Questions such as:

Who had reason to want to see General Custer discredited or otherwise nullified?

Who had the most constant contact with the hostile, non-treaty tribes?

Who had access to the most technically advanced weapon of the day, and the resources to move them at will?

Why was there never an inquiry into the actions of Major Marcus Reno and Captain Frederick Benteen?

Why do none of the Ordinance Department records, U. S. Government purchase records, or National Archive records list all the Henry rifles' serial numbers?

And last, what questions was George Custer asking about the Bureau of Indian Affairs?

All these questions point to the Federal government, the Bureau of Indian Affairs and the Grant Administration.

Conclusion -

Two significant events resulted from this tragic incident. First, the investigations into the dealings of William Belknap were stopped. The second was the answer to the death of Custer, which was an era of unrestricted slaughter of the Plains Indians and within a few years; a decade long struggle would come to a bloody end. The complete subjugating of the American natives was accomplished and few would ever question the death of George Armstrong Custer.

- Sources Used -
Adams, Linda, Emory Hackman; The Henry Rifle
Graham, W. A.; The Custer Myth
Parrett, Bryon: Last Stands

Wert, Jeffery D.; The Controversial Life of George Armstrong Custer
* * * * * *

Washington D. C. National Archive, Ordinance Records; December 30, 1863

Accelerated Intellect

Allow me to introduce myself, Quincy Wycliffe. Dr. Quincy Wycliffe M.D., PhD, D.Sc. the Director of the Molecular Chemistry Department at the St. Gabriel Molecular Scientific Research Center here in St. Gabriel. Or perhaps I should say former Director of the aforementioned department. I'm sure after the truth surfaces in what will likely be dubbed the St. Gabriel incident, I shall not only not be the head of this or any department, I doubt I will even be a free man.

I do wish for there to be some record for posterity's sake, something for the layperson. Something besides the scientific notes and recorded data that my experiments produced, something more than the record of a mere experiment gone awry. I want my desire to improve the human race to be realized by whoever may run across this obscure record. Lord knows the authorities will scrutinize my official one. It is in their hands now. My colleagues gasping at what they learn.

Of course you will hear the usual mumblings – that is natural in any human endeavor, mumblings by ignorant, hide-bound, jealous colleagues who question anything new or original. And had I not gotten side tracked with Smithy, I would still be in my lab analyzing and cataloguing the results of my latest experiments.

My latest experiment . . . I suppose, in a way, was Smithy. Smithson Abernathy - a unique young lad indeed. I first met young Smithson at the University Library of Bio-Chemical Research, which seemed an unlikely place for such a character. I mean Smithy looked quite out of place, dressed as he was, among the stuffed shirts and academic highness that surrounded him. But there he sat, several books opened as he took notes.

Had I not noticed one particular book, I most likely would not feel the need to write this now. The book in question was Identifying, Modifying and Utilization of Bio-Chemical Anomalies, by Woodley Bernstein. My God, I thought, where did he find this? You see this book, I thought – felt sure – had been banned from every University in the country. Of course, a simpleton like Smithson Abernathy knew nothing of the history of Woodley Bernstein or of bio-chemical anomalies. Smithson surely knew nothing of Dr. Woodley Bernstein's association with Albert Hoffman and the little known Hoffman-Bernstein experiments.

All Smithson Abernathy knew was he wanted to write. He had hundreds, if not thousands, of pages of hand written material. Unfortunately for Smithson, he had very little education. Oh, he had graduated from high school and had some minor degree. But as is so often the case in our modern age, he was graduated only to satisfy some quota on some registrar's desk.

He gained the titles without much else. No use of grammar or punctuation. No real writing skills. Couldn't spell syntax, which to Smithy was what sounded good. But he had a burning desire and was so damned determined.

I suppose that should count for something. One thing Smithy did have was imagination. Imagination and self-awareness. You see, Smithson Abernathy was mildly psychotic. Sometimes, not so mildly, and to confound matters he not only didn't take his prescribed medication regularly, but sometimes self medicated with illicit drugs.

Ah Smithson, my delusional young friend, if only you would have paid heed to my words, we both would be as before.

Be that as it may, when I noticed the copy of Identifying, Modifying and Utilization of Bio-Chemical Anomalies and the most recent copy of The Journal of Neuroscience among Smithy's clutter, I was compelled to speak.

"Some very interesting reading you have there, young man."

I suppose that Smithy was in the midst of some sort of elation phase of his condition because those few words were all it took. It was as if I had opened the flood gate to his mind. I stood there somewhat amused at this seemingly ignorant, near destitute young lad expounding on a subject he couldn't possibly grasp until . . . until he reached the subject of the "Breakthrough" column in The Journal of Neuroscience.

This article postulated that an extensive test on a group of writers would show a common down-regulation of the 5-HT2A receptor in the brain. Suddenly Smithson's intentions shined bright as a beacon. Of course Smithson Abernathy knew nothing of 5-HT2A receptor; in fact I doubted he had ever heard of neurotransmitters. He had no understanding of this article beyond being aware of having both psychological difficulties and a desire to write.

When I expressed obvious surprise at his perception and self-awareness a question and answer session ensued. As I struggled to explain to Smithson – in lay-persons terms – how neurotransmitters work, I was struck with a notion, a fantastic notion. What if the old Hoffman – Bernstein experiments were revived with the aid of modern techniques and improved methodologies? Ah, now we would truly be breaking new ground.

As I thought out loud Smithy continued his questions. I must give the lad credit, for his questions led directly to my first experiment. Before I knew it, Smithson and I were acquainted and he was working part time in my lab as an assistant. Of course, he was glad to submit himself to any experiment I suggested. The first experiment . . . a simple one really, check the level of 5-HT2A receptors in Smithson's brain. Even as I conducted these first experiments my mind raced forward to my next.

Now if there was indeed a link between his reduced 5-HT2A receptor levels and his mild psychosis and his desire to write, perhaps this would give weight to the old maxim that behind every form of genius does indeed lay some form of neurosis. How Smithy loved repeating this, as if his desire to write somehow legitimized his emotional shortcomings.

Be that as it may, the tests were conducted and Smithson showed the suspected reduced levels of the 5-HT2A receptor in his brain. It was at this time that my wildest theory became my greatest achievement. By this time I had taken leave of absence from my teaching and was spending days at a time in the lab. Such is the privilege for such a renowned name as Dr. Quincy Wycliffe. I assured all that I was on the verge of some earth shaking breakthrough.

For the sake of space and the readability of those of a less scientific background, I will condense and revise the nature of my findings to a more uninitiated form. First a quick over-view of the Hoffman – Bernstein experiments. Albert Hoffman, the scientist who synthesized LSD in 1938, Woodley Bernstein, who first suggested that neurotransmitters existed. These two fine, if not somewhat eccentric, thinkers proved beyond doubt that Lysergic acid diethylamide increased certain brain activities significantly. One of the most affected areas proved to be the cerebellum, which modulates output of other brain systems. Of course in Hoffman's day there was no method to activate or deactivate genes that control certain neurotransmitters. Oh, Dale's Principle – that is, the Cree-Lox reclamation process shined new light on this idea. I threaten to descend into technical jargon, forgive me, but this was the key to my revolutionary new theory. If the many side effects of Lysergic acid diethylamide could be eliminated, or controlled – through the stabilizing of certain neurotransmitters – the cerebral cortex could be stimulated and the results recorded.

I stood on the brink. I only needed a willing subject. In Smithson Abernathy I found that subject. First of course there were the usual batteries of test – a wide variety of measurements on his motor and sensory function. Most important were several composite cognitive processing tests related to abstract thoughts. These go far beyond the usual intelligence quotions test. But the big step, the monumental gain was the discovery of the Q-37 gene (as I so listed it). This gene controlled the site that released the 5-HT2A receptor. Of course it is important to note here that the use of Lysergic acid diethylamide, LSD hereafter, depletes this neurotransmitter and when depleted the effects of LSD are greatly reduced. Now, hypothetically, if one were to suppress the production of 5-HT2A in a subject with already low levels, well the subject could be given LSD, perhaps with little or no psycho-active side effects at all. The implications were fantastic.

I chose, somewhat expediently, to begin testing with Smithy at once. What discoveries would be made? What mysteries would be unraveled? The preliminary findings were fantastic! The Q-37 gene was successfully suppressed and the side effects of the LSD on Smithy were minimal. But even more fantastic were the effects on Smithy's brain. After only a month a Crowley Cortex inventory showed that Smithy had developed at least 10 billion new neurons in his cerebral cortex. Activity in all areas of young Smithson's brain increased at an exponential rate.

By summer Smithson had finished reading Identifying, Modifying and Utilization of Bio-Chemical Anomalies. Even more fantastic, he understood it. By the next fall I had him enrolled in St. Gabriel University for gifted students. It was about this time I began to spy a danger in the distance. Smithson had gained critical insight into the possibilities of this study and had long since demanded more than mere study subject status. What was I to do? Here was a young man who only a year ago was average or less in all cognitive and abstract thinking tests with an intelligence quotient of 98, who could now read a one thousand page neuropsychology manual in a few days – and understand it. More than understand it- memorize it!

Of course, I was pleased and fascinated by these stunning results. And it was very gratifying to see Smithson working so hard in the lab. It seems his fantastic progress had attracted the attention of Dr. Louis Sturgeon, President of the St. Gabriel Molecular Scientific Research

Center. A sort of mentor-ship formed and soon there was talk of an honorary degree for young Smithson.

But I was puzzled by all this. Smithson had developed a savvy that resided just beneath the surface. I suspected some sort of academic treachery afoot. Dr. Sturgeon began to speak in terms of the greatness of the achievements of St. Gabriel Molecular Scientific Research Center. Indeed the Center leads the country in fresh ideas and novel discoveries. But this new spring in Dr. Sturgeons step, and even more disturbing an underlying arrogance in Smithson Abernathy. What could it mean? Could Smithson be plotting to steal credit for my fantastic discoveries?

While all this was taking place I paid no attention to the latest construction renovations at the College. St. Gabriel is a sprawling complex and some sort of work goes on there often. One day I was on the north side of the campus and noticed a rather large building near completion. It was then that I remembered the strange whispers about some unknown project directed by Dr. Louis Sturgeon himself. There standing and talking to a well-dressed man in a hard hat was Dr. Sturgeon and, of all people, Smithson Abernathy.

As fate would have it, this structure, in fact, was the – as of yet, unnamed – Cognitive Acceleration Lab. It was rumored that Smithson was influencing Dr. Sturgeon on the naming of this new project. Unbelievable! In less than two years young Smithy had at least doubled his scores on every imaginable cognitive, intelligence or abstract thinking test. He was on the verge of earning an honorary PhD at a major university and now . . . now, Smithson Abernathy was influencing the president of a major institution of higher learning.

Alas, we were at a crossroads. There was no going back really. Like a snowball on some infinite snowy slope, Smithy had become a force of his own.

I could restrain myself no longer. I was finally able to corner Smithson, by himself, at lunch. I had planned to put some very pointed questions directly to Smithson, but upon our meeting my attention was quickly arrested by the many electrodes attached to his head. He greeted me with much excitement as he expounded on the ongoing experiment.

I sat in stunned amazement as he related to me the results of his latest Crowley Cortex Inventory. I listened with disbelief as I learned Smithson's cerebral cortex now contained an estimated sixty-billion neurons, twice that of the normal human brain. But the stunning revelations of the day had only begun.

I had been able to corner Smithy only because I learned he had developed a taste for foreign cuisine. I discovered his favorite restaurant. The restaurant, Mario's Meals-A-Many, was a multi-cultural eatery. It boasted over one hundred and thirty international cuisines. As I sat there lost in Smithson's fantastic story, we were interrupted by Mario, the owner.

Smithson turned, smiling and replied, "Me aligro de verte, que es de tu vida?" A short conversation ensued and in a moment Smithson turned to me and asked, "What can I get you Quincy?" Quincy was it, so now I was Quincy, was I?

With a civility I was far from truly possessing, I addressed Mario, "Me da un café."

Mario nodded and in hurried Spanish told Smithson he would send Gerza over. It seemed all this was happening at once. As if I was hearing Smithson speaking on in the background, my train of thought was being divided between Smithson's sudden familiarity with me and his new and remarkable command of Espanola.

As I pondered this, Gerza, a waiter dressed in traditional Turkish Bedouin style greeted Smithson and me. Well what happened then left me shaken. Smithson and Gerza began a conversation in Arabic. I sat in stunned silence as they conversed. While they still conversed my coffee was delivered. The surprises continued as I asked, "So you speak Arabic as well?" As I studied Smithson's face he began a dissertation on linguistics.

"Well Quincy, if I may call you that, it's not actually Arabic, not in the true sense of the word. It is what is known as "Ayancik" locally. Well locally to Gerza. You see, it is a mix of sorts, a bastardized mix of Arabic and Farsi, a terribly difficult dialect for either an Arab or Persian to . . "Stop it, Smithson. Stop it!" I realized I had pounded the table with my fist. I saw surprise register on Smithson's face. At this I sought to regain my composure.

"Quincy, what on earth is the matter?" Smithson studied me with an air of scrutiny, and I realized I was trembling.

I quickly regained my composure as best I could. "The recent pressures, Smithson, please forgive me . . . please."

"Yes, yes of course, Dr. Wycliffe. It is completely understandable."

I sat holding my face in my hands when Smithson offered me two small tablets for my tension. Without thinking I took them and washed them down with a drink of my coffee.

As Smithson and I talked I soon realized my tension was gone. And, as if he had read my mind quickly addressed my fears as far as any academic treachery was concerned. Suddenly I was struck by the fact that I had not yet mentioned the subject I had wished to discuss with young Smithy. As my surprise registered, it was compounded, yet again . . . "I can see, Professor Wycliffe, by the look on your face, that you are unaware of my newly developed, shall we say, intuition."

"Smithson, what on earth is happening here? What have you been up to these last weeks? Why have I not been able to reach you?"

"For one, my good doctor, I've been advising Dr. Sturgeon on the naming of the latest St. Gabriel project. I am pleased to report – and please keep this to yourself as it is not yet official– the new lab will be named the Q-Cliffe building! That is for short of course. It will officially be designated the Quincy Wycliffe Cognitive Acceleration Center.

I hardly knew what to answer. Here I was suspecting treachery, now Smithson tells me this. "Why Smithson, I . . . I . . . I hardly know what to say."

"Say nothing Quincy, you deserve this. You have changed the course of human history. More than that, Dr. Wycliffe, you have changed my life."

I was touched by Smithson's words and felt a strange warmth growing inside me.

"Dr. Wycliffe, if someone of my limited mental and educational background can make such advances in so short a time, what are the implications? What effects would our experiments have on someone of already advanced mental capabilities?"

I pondered Smithson's idea and for some reason it seemed remarkably funny. I chuckled a bit and remember a distinct look of puzzlement come over Smithson's face.

It was at this time I began to feel a somewhat pleasant feeling of stimulated euphoria. As we continued to speak it increased until I found myself laughing out loud. I do remember Smithson looking at his watch and it prompting me to comment that time is only a man- made concept. At this comment I saw Smithson's look of puzzlement turn into a look of worry.

I also distinctly remember - for some reason I could not possibly grasp at the time – I stood, spread my arms wide and proclaimed loudly, "See this stage here filled with humans, they have no concept of what time really is. They sit there on their complacent asses while the world passes them by ..." I also remember laughing loudly as I wave my arms in all directions.

At this Smithy quickly stood, I suppose to restrain me. I do remember seeing a steak knife on the table beside us. The patrons at this table were staring at me with a look of shock as they slowly rose and backed away.

This is the last thing I remember that doesn't come to me as if through a haze. Here I can speak only of what I suspect happened, piecing together a story from the few facts I have gathered.

I do hope that Smithson will survive for his wounds were extremely serious. For the fact he lives now I can thank Gerza. For the fact that I am now confined to the maximum security ward of the St. Gabriel Psychiatric Hospital, I can thank Smithy.

You see the two tablets I ingested were something Smithson had recently created. It seems he saw this as a perfect opportunity to test his newly developed theory. Were LSD given with something that could naturally neutralize the 5-HT2A receptor, why you could artificially create the conditions we had achieved by suppressing the Q-37 gene.

I had warned Smithson that mimicking a gene's effects with a compound is not the same as altering the gene. I do know in some of our preliminary tests this theory worked, but only as long as the Q-37 suppressor that was in the system counteracted the effects of the LSD. In every case the LSD out lasted the added suppressor and left the test subject under the psycho-active effects of LSD. Some unknown factor always confounded the suppressor of the LSD. We were never able to determine what the unknown factor was.

I suspect that Smithson came to believe he had found the confounding factor and had successfully neutralized it.

I am sure something along these lines is what caused this fiasco.

"Oh, Dr. Quincy . . ."

That damned orderly again, "Yes, what now?"

"Time for your treatment doctor, I do hope you will be more cooperative today ..."

The Testing of Restraint

A Texas prison is a very strange world and gives way to very strange problems. I should have known from the start where my problem with Harold would eventually lead… a violent physical confrontation. I could have saved myself almost four years of useless frustration if I had just slugged him in the beginning. But being committed to doing things differently than I had in the past, I was determined to use our system to deal with this rogue. This only compounded the original problem. Foolish as it was, I do not regret my efforts to use our system because I believe doing so is what separates us from the lower primates. But neither do I regret taking the course of action I finally took. I learned a very important lesson, sometimes our system just doesn't work and you must be prepared to consider other, less conventional alternatives. Now some will say this represents a step backward, and indeed, in a way it does. But physical violence was used – as it must always be – as a last resort.

The details of what lead to the confrontation are many and varied. The main one I suspect is that Harold is a psyche patient and I am a bit of one myself. That, and being Caucasian are the only similarities we share.

As the result of a stupid argument in March of 2001, Harold and I would be at each other's throats until our final finish in December of 2004. During this time I made several peace offerings, which were coldly spurned or accepted and then later forgotten. The situation finally degenerated into a protracted psychological war of attrition and countless dirty tricks were pulled. By both of us. I was at a major disadvantage, in that I had a great deal to lose. Many times I would be waiting to see parole or waiting on an answer when Harold would try to provoke a fight. I would, in turn (being a master of the practical joke) do something to really piss him off. If he attacked me, I reasoned, I had a chance of explaining my actions. But as I came up for parole every year Harold was presented with many good opportunities to test me. But his best tries were reserved for when I was waiting on a marriage seminar – the most important event in prison. If I maintained a good disciplinary record I could attend every six months. I being happily married aggravated Harold's insecurities so my seminars became a natural target. He tried every manner of treachery and foul play to rob me of any peace of mind he could.

Knowing me as I do I look back on this period with some amazement that I restrained my barbaric nature as long as I did. Often times I remembered the words of Thucydides, the 5th century B.C. Greek general who said, "Of all the manifestations of power, restraint most impresses men". How true his words are, except my restraint was missed by Harold, who continued to interpret it as weakness or fear. Another of his favorite tactics was to try to provoke a confrontation on my commissary day. As we lived in different dorm buildings we had different store days. It is much easier to take someone to jail with you on "their" store day. And so it was on a store day that he was able to provoke me to give him a shot at the title. It is customary to get the gatehouse officer's signature on your commissary slip. To get to the gatehouse I had to walk past the weight machine. There at the weight machine were several big black inmates pumping iron and one medium sized white boy who I heard say, "That's him there", indicating me. I looked around and Harold had a stupid look on his face. No doubt he was slandering my good name again as he had done so often (Another of his tactics). What was I this time I wondered . . . a clansman, a snitch, a child molester? I said loud enough for everyone at the weight machine to hear me that a "man" will speak to another man's face. I walked past and was told by the gatehouse officer to return in ten minutes. Well I had already made the decision for the hundredth time, enough is enough. I returned to my dorm, changed foot wear and stretched a few muscles. Then I sat on my bunk to pray a prayer I've prayed many times in my life, "Father let me avoid this violence, if not, let my aim be true". I think by the time I was on my way back to the gatehouse I could have let the matter lay had fate not intervened. As it turned out the commissary line had formed almost all the way back to the weight machines so further contact was inevitable.

I had some size on Harold, but I also had ten years of hard living on him as well. I had broken the 3rd metacarpal of my left hand the year before and the bone had not been set right and my hand healed up partially crippled, so my blinding left jab was no more. I've been into various forms of Martial Arts almost all my life. Despite my tattered physical condition and advanced age I can still take care of myself. Harold was stout and hit the iron regularly. I had once seen him pull one of his own teeth.

Not everyone can do that. I knew he didn't fear pain. And as he had made fun of the Martial Arts on many occasions, I intended to test his tolerance to pain and perhaps help him with another tooth.

When I got to the end of the line another remark was made. I basically called him out and to my surprise he stepped out. He walked right into a front kick to his groin. He jumped back telling me, "You kick like a girl!", hoping, I think, to get it back on a verbal level. Not to be, I was already in the mode and I had thought of this moment for way too long. I threw a leading round-house kick at his head, which he barely ducked. He let me get too close and I buried the toe of my brogan in his thigh, then again in his chest. He was backed to the weight machines where I slipped a good right cross through his defenses and landed a shot squarely on his jaw. Ah, the sound that made . . . music I tell you! Anyway, he then grabbed me so I thumbed him in the eye, but he partially dodged it and pushed me back over the bench rest. I went all the way to the ground, but pulled him with me. I was pinned down, but was able to hold him in position and with my free leg executed a Bedinski heel smash to his forehead, twice, which ended the conflict. By this time people were calling out, warning about the police. As we were breaking it up a Lieutenant walked by looking at us crazy, but said nothing. I got back in line and a friend looked at me and asked, "How did that feel?" I thought for a moment and answered, "Good, damn good."

Harold never bothered me again. He later told me he was being harassed by a "tuffy" after learning he had made parole. Then much to my surprise he added, "I guess I had that coming." I then asked him if he had ever heard of Thucydides.

Axmehak: A Study in Axiotransmendacitism

Axiotransmendacitism, or Axmehak as the word was originally formulated, is a linguistic anomaly if ever there was one.

When one goes in search of this word's history they should be prepared. First of all for scant information. Secondly for conflicting stories that reach as far back as ancient Babylon.

In fact, of the many dictionaries researched for this survey only a few make references to "Axmehak", fewer still offer a definition of axiotransmendacitism.

One, the long out-of-print Edinburgh University Advanced College Dictionary of 1759, offers this definition: "1. the use of sarcasm to pervert the truth. 2. The use of satire to confuse or baffle 3. To compound fraud with sarcasm".

The International Heritage Scottish Enlightenment Dictionary of 1770 definition is no more precise: "1. To indict by dubious text. 2. An invention marked by sarcasm. 3. A rude satire foisted upon the unwary".

The inception of "Axmehak" is believed by some authorities to date back to ancient Babylon. The Akkadian language offers clues to the first use of a form of this word.

Babylonian legend claims the scholar Akmed coined the term "axmehak", which referred to the language the Babylonians tried to use after the builders of the Tower of Babel were confused by God.

Axmehak is roughly translated to mean, "Truth transformed into fallacy". According to Archibald Story in his out of print and impossible to find book, Questionable Stone Etchings, he asserts that Akmed was stoned to death by an angry mob who misunderstood the word "axmehak" to mean, "Kill the messenger."

The next historical appearance of "axmehak" it seems was 450 B.C. in a text written by Aristippus, founder of the Cyrenaic school. He was a philosopher and historian who became obsessed with the historical origin of "axmehak". His application of "axikhiasma" was incorporated into the classic Greek language for some time.

But according to Bullard Cornburg's self-published and controversial, "The Fall of Cyrene", Aristippus eventually had a nervous collapse over a suit brought against the Cyrenaic school for using a word "axikhiasma", that was deemed offensive to Athena, the goddess of wisdom. The Cyrenaic school was closed and Aristippus' "axikhiasma" was removed from the Greek language.

It seems "axikhiasma" was later revived by the philosopher Marcus Tullius Cicero in 72 B.C. The new form of axikhiasma was "axtramedatism". But like Akmed and Aristippus before him, the use of this word seemed a curse. In Roman text "axtramedatism" was translated "The use of truth to lie to a fool."

A local statesman and politician, Catiline – who just by chance was plotting against Caesar – took Cicero's interpretation as a direct ridicule of his recent speech to the senate. A political feud ensued until the death of Catiline in 62 B.C.

According to Horace Featherman's "Roman Mounds", the death of Cicero a few years later brought about another change in axtramedatism. As the feud between the two statesmen had caused several embarrassing scenes, Caesar had his head scholar redefine the word to mean "a quarrelsome exchange". Its spelling was changed, again to, "conaximedatism."

Conaximedatism remained a part of the Roman language for the next four-hundred years. Then according to author and former psychiatric patient Napoleon Bonaparte, Augustine, while bishop of Hippo in A.D. 410, had his head scribe research the word. His scribe, Piazza Pistole, also known as the "Fool of Bolona", re-translated the word "conaximedation" to mean, "God is a jester." Pistole was excommunicated and eventually killed.

Conaximedation does not surface again until 1540. While in a library, Ignatius of Loyola discovers an essay written by none other than . . . Piazza Pistole. In a final attempt to set straight the definition of "conaximedation", Ignatius commissions a church secretary to research and re-define the word. The secretary, Signore Mucho el-Mierda, gave the word its present day spelling of "Axiotransmendacitism". And defined the word to mean "Anyone who jests in the name of God will die."

Unfortunately for Signore Mucho el-Mierda, he did just that. He died a violent death at the hands of the Jesuits.

And so finally in 1801, Peter Mark Roget discovered the word, "Axiotranemendacitism". So intrigued he became with this strange word and its history, he veered away from his first love of science and medicine and became involved in a lifetime of secretaryships with several learned societies. His search led him to see a need for clarity and forcefulness of expression. For the next fifty-one years he labored, and in 1852, when he was seventy-three years old, published, Roget's International Thesaurus.

Historical rumor says that Roget's contemporaries – William Cullen, Alexander Primus and David Hume – all were afraid to associate with Roget as he researched "Axiotransmendacitism."

Later, Sir James Young Simpson, while high on chloroform, claimed . . . "axiotransmendacitism," the greatest word ever spoken". Simpson later commits suicide in prison while suffering from chloroform addiction.

Oh, a footnote on Roget's Thesaurus, it does not contain any reference to axiotransmendacitism. In the end Roget became disillusioned with the history of the word. Perhaps sparing himself an unfortunate end. Axiotransmendacitism: A word still without a clear definition.

Sources used:
Bonapart, Napoleon; Fool of Bolona
Cornburg, Bullard; The Fall of Cyrene
Featherman, Horace; Roman Mounds
Pistole, Piazza; Confussa Axikhiasma
Story, Archibald; Questionable Stone Etchings

Dig Not a Hole

Well, here I sit in group therapy doing a writing exercise. When I asked what I was supposed to write about, I was told, "whatever is on your mind . . ." Is he kidding? He can't be serious. I'm a neurotic, bi-polar manic. I suffer from delusions of grandeur . . . I'm paranoid . . . surely he jests. Or perhaps he is doing a detailed study on psychosis. Or perhaps this is a trick . . . a clever ploy to see what I write. Ask me to just write what's on my mind thinking I will write something other than what is on my mind that can be analyzed, but the subtle truth is he really does want what is on my mind. Ah ha! I now have this figured out. It's a detailed study to see if, in fact, all writers are psychotic. They say all forms of genius are rooted in some form of psychosis. By those standards this could be some sort of entrance exam. I look around and these other people look no more stable than I. Look at them all. Scribbling away or sitting there scratching their heads. I doubt any of them have figured out what is going on here. They just keep writing away not realizing their thoughts will be picked apart. Come to think of it, they may be onto something. Introduce this test to all who think they need this. They could assign a certain status according to the level of psychosis one demonstrates. Actually cultivate neurotic behavior and channel it into an art. Yes, that's it. Make psychotic writing into an art form . . . Oh wait, I have already done that. That's what got me here.

Oh, what's that . . .? Write a poem? What the hell is he talking about, write a poem? I'm already writing something. Oh, I see, yes, he figured out what I am doing. Clever bastard, trying to throw me off balance. I'll not fall for this. Let's see . . . Need something to pass as a poem. Anything will do. People will accept any kind of rubbish as poetry. Like time, poetry is a man-made concept . . . Let's see . . .

> Blank Mind . . .
> I just used up all I had.
> So here I sit, nothing left to say.
> Can't be the end . . . They say you can always dig deeper.
> Deeper, deeper, deeper . . .
> Deeper still . . . Isn't that how graves are dug?

There you have it, a work of art. I'll give this malarkey some fancy title. "Dig Not A Hole" Ah yes, the great work by So 'n So, "Dig Not a Hole", a deeply spiritual account of a man's descent into the innermost recesses of his soul. Ah, the critics will go crazy over it. Then, when they proclaim it a great work, I will expose them for the fools that they are. That's not a great work you imbecile, it was me killing time in some stupid therapy class. Ha, ha, what do you have to say to that, Mr. Art Critic? Caught in your own trap! Dig not a hole without filling it back up, lest you fall in it! Oh, hold on . . . Dig? Dig, dig, dig . . . Dig deeper . . . My God! "Dig Not a Hole" is a work of art. I've been tricked into creating a "something"! Who knows what obscure bits of prattle will become tomorrow's archive treasures? Hell, look at our great Constitution. It was written by a group of renegade winos, and pot heads (Actually, opium heads) on the run from other countries. Just consider our founding fathers for a moment. Washington was a bleeding Freemason for God's sake. And how about that old fart, Ben Franklin? What an old lecher he was! And what about the Gettysburg Address? Lincoln's own words were "that will never scower . . ." Scower? Scower my ass, what the hell is that supposed to mean? If that's not psychotic, what is? Genius or psychotic? But when you look closely at many of our greatest historical figures, they were just as crazy. Ol' Churchill coined the phrase "Black dogs of depression". And Machiavelli? Ever read any of his crap? Prince Machiavelli? More like Prince Loon-O!

Oh, what's that? Time's up? Stop writing? Yeah, right. Now you want to silence me. Not quite the same when someone figures you out, huh? No thank you sir, I'll not be silenced. What? Disturbing the class? This group? Ha, ha! It is to laugh. The only one I'm disturbing is you. You can't stand it because I have figured you out. Thought I wouldn't catch on to your little scam, did you? Well, now you know better. Oh yeah, that's right, make a phone call. Don't dare to argue such a weak position in front of the class. Who are you calling, the C. I. A.? What are you going to tell them, I'm a subversive for talking bad about Ben Franklin? You stuffed shirts are all the same. Sit high on your pompous asses hiding behind your spectacles, then when somebody catches you in one of your games, you change the subject or ask them to write a poem. Then, when your subject refuses to give quarter, you fake a phone call. I'll bet no one is even on the other end of the line. Yeah, keep looking crazy at me while you move your lips. What a fake old bastard you are. Got to give it to him, he's faking a good phone call. Some may even fall for it. Now he has the rest of the class looking at me. I'll pay no attention. But first . . . (I just thumbed my nose at that old billy goat!) Now, where was I? Oh yes, Nietzsche. The guy that thought he could disprove God's existence. Died in a nut house. Well duh, why do you think they call him God? What a loser!

Ah, some new students. Must be, they are wearing white. Wherever they are from, they grow them big. Well, they seem to be working their way over here. What? Can't you see I'm writing? What, that old poof? Pay no attention to him. Just between you and me, I don't think he is all there. Do what? Escort you? What? You don't know your way around. How did you find this class room? Excuse me fellow, but if you don't give me a little room, I'm going to have a panic attack on you and your friends. Oh, is that so, you want to try? Oh yeah? That's right, spread out. How about a what? How about I shove a thumb in your eye socket, fatso? Relax? Relax my ass, get away from me and I will . . . I'm warning you. (Thump!) How'd you like that? Hey, get that thing away from me Bozo. I tell you, I don't do needles. Ouch! Let go, you big buffoon. What wazh that shtuf . . .? You shnuke baslards . . . Tink I'm gonna puke . . . Oooh . . . Slurned th slights out . . . ZZZZZZ . . .

The Sparring Partner

Jerry was one of those people who, at first glance, I knew was just not the average guy. I met Jerry while I was incarcerated and assigned to one of the many Texas Prison ID units. Our common interest in writing was what led us to our first conversation. He was very well mannered and intelligent, though I got the feeling there was much more to this fellow than a first glance would reveal. Using my 6' height as a measuring stick, he was at least 6' tall. At approximately 190-lbs, he was in very good physical condition. His most impressive feature had to be his eyes. Pale blue and had a certain . . . reptilian quality. Few people's eyes convey the strange distance Jerry's eyes did. I later learned the reason for the distant stair in his eyes and must admit that I wasn't that surprised. In fact, the look made sense. His arms and upper torso were covered with tattoos. His back and rib cage were covered with tattoos of Gothic women in various semi-erotic poses. He had a huge scull on his chest and stomach. His most interesting tattoo was a Cheshire cat on the back of his head. He was kind of a skin head and you could easily judge by the length of Jerry's hair where his mind was on any given day. The more it grew out the more "normal" Jerry seemed. When he was out of sorts with the world the first thing he did was shave his head so the cat would show. He said this was to demonstrate "irreverent humor", but the reasons were much more deeply rooted than he let on. Jerry and I also shared a common interest in the Martial Arts and that was how we got to know each other well. Schooled in American Free-Style Karate, he was one hell of a sparring partner - very fast and hard as a rock. When I kicked him barefoot, it hurt my foot. I dislocated toes, and once broke the middle toe of my right foot sparring with Jerry. He could read an opponent with amazing accuracy. We would often spar on a whim and he could tell, as well as I, what level we were sparring on. Whether it was playing, slap boxing, light or full contact. I don't recall either of us ever verbalizing what level we were on. We just did it. We talked often and through our talks I came to realize that unlike my Martial Arts learning experience, Jerry had not absorbed any of the Martial Arts traditional philosophy such as improvement of self or control of fear and anger. To him the Martial Arts was a means to an end, to protect and enforce his idealism. An idealism fueled by the rabid hatred his tattooed carcass housed. At times he tried to rationalize his hate mongering. Some of his arguments were based on fact, others . . . is anyone's guess.

It is certain that not everyone who is locked up in this country is guilty and it is also certain that many are. There is a rule one must accept when incarcerated if you are to retain your sanity and that is to not concern yourself with other's offences. As far as offences go, there are some that stand out so egregiously as to mark the offender a pariah. In general population, few detainees there are who have no contemporaries at all. There are a few, but for the most part, everyone has some contact with others. There is no telling who you might find yourself talking to, or even liking. Learning that Jerry was a serial rapist and murderer was a fact I had a hard time with. At least then I understood the distant look in his eyes.

Jerry was a truly gifted writer and as with any writer, you can get a sense of being no matter what the subject matter. But it took no great effort of reading between the lines of Jerry's work to sense his ongoing love affair with his own mortality. This, I think, was the product of his death wish, or perhaps its source. In many of our talks we delved deep into the psychology of any number of subjects and people, even ourselves. When we used ourselves as subjects, Jerry would always steer our analysis toward me, always resisting any deep examination of himself. I latched onto this fact tenaciously. The more he resisted, the harder I pursued the matter. We both knew I was doing this and the only reason he let this continue as long as he did was because he knew I genuinely cared about him as a person. But even this would only take me so far because concern for your fellow man was a concept almost totally foreign to him.

I probably learned more about Jerry's hidden past from what he wouldn't tell me, than he learned about me from what I would freely tell him. I learned that the only person in his life he ever really cared about was his abusive father. The subject of a mother he would not address except in his writing, couched in simile and metaphor. I learned through his writing-and questions he would not answer- that the only girl he ever loved had died in some accidental blaze. I found that pondering the source of this fire and the unknown circumstances bothered the hell out of me.

We all suffer from some degree of neurosis, healthy or otherwise, and from time to time certain events will generate reactions from us all. This was the case after an inmate had killed his cell mate by strangling him with a handmade garrote. Of course the unit was abuzz with talk about this tragedy and I soon realized Jerry was obsessed with this event. Time after time our conversation would become strained to the point of conflict because of his constant referral to this blasted killing. He wanted to believe so bad that the unit was on the brink of a race war because of it, and when I pointed out that the victim and perpetrator were of the same race, he only became more agitated.

His fatalistic views of the world began to get the better of me so I began to shy away from Jerry. I noticed that when he would come around he would be in one extreme state or another. It seemed he would either be subdued and consciously trying to control his hate and death mongering, or he would try to deliberately draw me into an argument on race, or philosophy, or any subject he knew we drastically differed on. Whatever the conflict within his being, I could feel it was reaching critical mass. I had no desire to be around Jerry when it did. Not long after this a very regrettable incident took place that radically altered our friendship, if our contact could ever have been rated a friendship.

Though I was to the point of actively avoiding any direct conversation with Jerry sometimes contact is unavoidable, like at recreation time. He approached me in one of his more affable moods and addressed our recent lack of regular conversation. I calmly explained that our recent conversation had become a source of distress for me and life in prison is stressful enough as it is. I thought this was an explanation anyone could clearly understand. In reply Jerry told me that the only reason he expends so much effort on my behalf is because he sees such potential in me.

I took great offense to this. I asked, what exactly did he mean? As I spoke my next words, part of me struggled to restrain them, for I knew my mouth was about to say something my logic did not condone. I sarcastically told him I had no potential to slash a street walkers' throat as I engaged in doggy style sex with her and things quickly came to a very dangerous boiling point. Jerry had not told me of this aspect of his offense, but knew I had heard of it, and sadly, it was a point of pride with him. I will never forget the look on his face and I knew that I had offended his malignant pride. He stepped back into a stance and offered a serious challenge. I assumed an open stance and asked him if this was what this was all about. I told him if he wanted a match, a real match, why not just initiate one. He didn't have to go through all this bullshit. He should just fire on me, as he knows I will defend myself to the best of my ability.

We stood for many seconds sizing up our situation. I could feel the advantage of my control of fear and anger and I could sense that he believed, I believed myself to have some hidden advantage. To this day I believe this was the only thing that kept me from having to defend myself in what would have been a very serious match. Strange as it may seem, it was as if mixed with his hatred of what he believed I stood for, there was a tinge of sadness at what was a sure break in any future interaction. When his look suddenly softened slightly I took the opportunity to tell Jerry our views of life were just too different. As kindly as I could in such a strange situation I offered Jerry a match on any level he wanted. I told him we could test our martial skills without having to taint the match with our personal beliefs. He looked at me very strangely and kind of waved at me and walked off.

Things were very different between us after that. We never talked again, though a couple of times we made eye contact and if I thought Jerry was about to speak to me it gave me the creeps really bad. We lived in the same dorm and an attack on a sleeping man is not uncommon. The day after our confrontation I taped three new, freshly sharpened pencils under the little table by my bunk, and then actively practiced reaching for them in my sleep.

A short time later the unit underwent a shake up and most everyone's housing was changed.

Later I heard that as the result of an attack on another inmate, Jerry was transferred to another unit. Upon hearing this, I felt a degree of relief. From time to time Jerry's writing would show up in various publications that are common to incarcerated writers. Reading his work I could only shake my head, for his morbid view of the world had not changed one iota. Still . . . Jerry was one hell of a sparring partner.

Footnote by Jack Crowsey:

The story you just read is no work of fiction. I was there and had several confrontations and close calls with this serial rapist, confessed murderer and one man crime wave.

Connections Amis

Mohammed carefully made the connection. The French made Sevelor remote control garage door opener was now connected to both the dry cell battery and the 25 watt light bulb that would act as the detonator for the several pounds of Pirodex they had collected. Looking over his shoulder was Mirsky, his unlikely conspirator. "Are you not afraid of what they say about the Sevelor's wide frequency band?" Mohammed paused and looked up. "It will only be activated seconds before it is used, there will be no problem." Mirsky wondered to himself how he could be taking part in such a plan as Mohammed had devised – to kill their two best friends. Build a bomb, plant it and blow to bits the only two people either Mohammed or he had ever been close to.

He stared out the window of the apartment into the darkness replaying the steps that lead to such an unlikely friendship that had formed in high school and to the situation he now found himself. Mirsky Goldstein, a Jewish exchange student had become best friends with a neo-Nazi skin head, a black gangster and the son of Arab immigrants.

The four were drawn to each other because of their lack of social skills. The misbegotten foursome was such a novelty that they all found acceptance. Amidst the confusion of the American High School experience they leaned on each other. There was a time when the four were almost able to rise above the dysfunction of their respective families. Had they met earlier in life, their influence on each other might have made a difference – and had they not discovered drugs. It was fun at first, getting high and watching action movies. Then they discovered real money could be made with drugs. Soon reality began to blur. Ralph shaved his head, Leroy imagined himself as a "gangsta", Mohammed became a radical Muslim and Mirsky got religious. As the contrast increased so did the novelty of their friendship. Acceptance turned into real popularity. Then school ended and left the four to confront the real world. Mirsky felt regret for the lost good times.

"Mohammed, how have we come to this? Is there no other way?" Mohammed paused again looking up at his friend a bit sternly while running a hand over his beard. "Mirsky, we have been betrayed. Our plans, our ideals, our principals. Leroy wants the profits only for pleasure. He has poisoned Ralph's mind as well. Ralph protects Leroy only to serve his own interests. Much has changed since our days of friendship in school. Remember Mirsky, we only sell drugs to finance our plans. The money is critical to our struggle."

With that said Mohammed screwed the large threaded lid down. The project was complete. Five pounds of synthetic black powder incased in a piece of six inch cast iron pipe. He held it up for Mirsky's inspection. "There, you see, one connection and it is armed."

Meanwhile Leroy and Ralph sat in a tattered trailer house outside of town stuffing 9mm rounds into the magazines of the new Marline Camp Carbines they had recently purchased. They laughed as they discussed their plans. Leroy stood and looked the carbine over. "Now we parties good 'foe we go do this! Celebrate, cuz after it be done, we run the whole show." Ralph laughed as he chambered a round with a quick, crisp pull on the charging bolt.

"Say Leroy, I can't believe that fuck'n Moe would rather do politics bullshit than make money and get high."

"Fuck that rag head, he changed since high school. So has Mirsky. All that social injustice bullshit. Fuck all that noise. Hell, I don't need no-body tell'n me the world ain't fair. I knows the world ain't fair. But we got a good deal here. He want to go an piss it off build'n bombs. Bring heat down on our asses."

"That's some shit for sure, Leroy. A yid and a rag-head want'n to blow shit up over politics. I try to tell him, 'Moe, that's all politics is good for.' That's where Moe went wrong. First religion then fuck'n politics. Now he don't even want to get high anymore. But every time he got high he would start talkin that shit again. I'd tell him 'Moe, you aint Osama, you'll get your ass shot play'n them bullshit religious games.'

"Well, Ralph you right, he get his ass shot, and to-fuck'n-night!"

Later that night Mohammed and Mirsky sat in a wooded lot behind Leroy's ragged trailer. After a short time to let their eyes adjust to the darkness they started down a path of no return. They followed a small stream bed to the back of the brush covered lot where Leroy's trailer sat. Soon Mohammed was peering in a window. He counted on Leroy's and Ralph's music and partying to keep them distracted. He wasn't disappointed. He felt a surge of righteous indignation as he watched them pass the pipe. He gave a signal and Mirsky took up his position. Mohammed crept along the skirt of the trailer to the opening that had been made days before. In only a minute he was under the trailer. He would plant the bomb under the living room where Leroy and Ralph sat smoking and drinking. Only a bit farther . . . Mirsky gave the signal. Mohammed was directly under the living room.

Inside the trailer the partying continued. As the beer was guzzled and the crack pipe passed and the good old days were re-lived, Leroy spoke. "Say Ralph, think they be any way to deal with those dumb asses?"

Ralph sat for a moment thinking. "Damn Leroy, I wish there was. I mean I don't mind hit'n-em if we got to, but . . . I mean shit man, we did have some good times." Leroy reached for his cell phone.

"One try Ralph, one fuck'n try. Maybe Moe will listen, maybe we can cut a deal. We give them the south side. Hell, they is plenty to go round. If Moe will take it we aint got to do it. One try for old time sake."

Ralph thought for a moment. "Think he'll take it Roy?"

"He God-damn sure better, cuz if he don't you knows what time it is! Hell he can spend they money on whatever he wants. Just leave us the fuck alone."

Leroy picked up his cell phone and hit speed dial. As he did the micro-waves spread out in all directions. Some to the closest telephone wires that act as antennas, some up, up, up into the air to a communication satellite passing over head. Some to Mohammed's cell phone back at the car some distance away. Mohammed's phone emitted its usual ring tone.

Mohammed had just placed the bomb and made the critical connection when a random micro-wave struck the sensor on the Sevelor's receiver. In only a few nano-seconds it reacted and made the connection. A few more nano-seconds and the electricity from the dry cell battery was traveling through the wire to the 25 watt light bulb. As electrical resistance began to build the filament heated. More resistance, more heat. The filament heated to the point that the surrounding Pirodex reacted. As Mohammed made the connection his concentration was so intense his mind registered a snap within the casing he held in his hands. For only as long as it takes a micro-wave to travel Mohammed saw a bright light directly in front of his face.

Inside the trailer Leroy sat holding the cell phone. It seemed as if a loud noise accompanied the feel of the sofa being lifted. Ralph was reaching for the cooler when a piece of the cast iron casing tore his head from his shoulders.

The peaceful night silence was broken and the sky lit up as the trailer house was engulfed in a ball of fire. Mirsky felt an intense heat rush as he was blinded by a bright orange flame. The force of the explosion flung him through the air several yards. He landed in the creek with a splash. He was aware of a burning numbness throughout his body. Mostly he was aware of his utter blindness. He could feel the heat of the roaring flames as what was left of Leroy's trailer house was quickly consumed.

As he lay there in the creek there was a sharp contrast between the cool wetness of the water and the roaring inferno nearby. His consciousness slipped away as his mind drifted back in time. Back to a time before politics and religion. Back to a time with Mohammed and Leroy and Ralph. Back to a time and place, sitting with his friends, getting high and watching action movies. He watched a police chase scene not knowing the sirens were real and an ambulance was on the way.

A Dysfunctional Father

Sigmund Freud is generally considered to be the father of psychoanalysis; however his legacy is a bewildering mix of contradictions. He contributed much to our present-day understanding of psychology. He promoted healthier attitudes towards more humane treatment of children, mental patients and prisoners.

We now know that much of Freud's ground-breaking work was, unfortunately, tainted by his personal bias, bizarre imagination and an unusual impressionability. It is truly amazing that much of the mythology laid down for us by Sigmund Freud is still accepted as credible in the light of what we now know of the man.

Being a man of his time he subscribed to a good deal of the quackery that had preceded him. Much of his work was so outlandish as to border on the absurd. Just as many professional people who followed Freud, he was prone to believe in the fantastic.

If any one of several aspects of Sigmund Freud's personality is considered, serious questions begin to mount. Questions surrounding subjects such as his use of cocaine, his early mentor, Jean-Martin Charcot, and his belief in his own infallibility leads one to question why

Sigmund Freud still holds such an esteemed place in the world of psychiatry.

Even more disturbing is the effects of some of Freud's wild ideas on infantile sexuality, his obsession with incest and his theory of memory repression. There is reason to believe that one of the sources of influence on the overly impressionable young Freud was the popular plays of his day.

But first let us consider the impression left on Sigmund Freud by his early mentor, Jean-Martin Charcot.

In 1885, the young Freud studied under Charcot for a few months. The experience so impressed him that he changed his field of study from Neuropathology to Psychopathology. And so, Sigmund Freud, the father of psychoanalysis was born. It is telling that his mentor, Charcot, was judged harshly by many of his contemporaries. Charcot's theories and treatment were often referred to as "Charcot's Circus."

According to Edward Shorter in his <u>A History of Psychiatry</u>, Jean Martin-Charcot's theories, as well as much of his work, lacked any research and defied even basic common sense. Charcot was certain of the correctness of his own judgment. Both of these regrettable tendencies, it seems, were passed on to the impressionable young Freud.

There is on record instances of medical students actually helping patients escape from a ward of the mental hospital where Charcot was director. One patient was an attractive young female who Charcot was attracted to. Just as Charcot had strong tendencies for unethical behavior towards "attractive young female" patients, this would become a long standing mark of Freud's practice.

After Jean-Martin Charcot's death in 1893 many influential professionals in France who had accepted and promoted his work began to realize the bizarre nature of some of his theories and methodologies. Soon his work fell into disrepute, many of his ideas were refuted and the profession suffered a setback from which the country took decades to recover.

This would serve to be another similarity in the careers of the two men.

Until recently, Freud's pronouncements were considered substantially true despite the many oddities surrounding his ethics and methodology. Many of Freud's critics point to his extravagant use of cocaine.

Surely Sigmund Freud's frequent and lifelong use of cocaine stands out as one of the strangest details of his career.

The new drug – as we know it today – synthesized in 1860, was proclaimed a miracle by Freud. As a medical researcher he was a major force behind the popularization of cocaine for almost any ailment. Here again we find an example of Freud being influenced by the illogical.

In this case it was Wilhelm Fleiss who recommended cocaine as a treatment for a rather dubious diagnosis called "nasal reflex neurosis." In fact Fleiss actually performed surgery on several people, including Sigmund Freud for this imagined condition. The fact that Freud would go under the knife on the advice of Wilhelm Fleiss shows just how terribly impressionable he was.

In "Freudian Fallacy", E. M. Thornton argues that all of Freud's theories were products of cocaine hallucinations. Other followers of Freudian theory contest this assertion. But many of Freud's letters to his friend, Wilhelm Fleiss, are filled with obsessive concern over his nose and its secretions. Freud applied cocaine as a curative. No doubt the cocaine was responsible for his runny nose to begin with. This did not detour his continued use or his giving cocaine to his patients.

It is all too clear that Sigmund Freud used cocaine on a regular basis as well as freely dispensing it. More serious than his vice of cocaine use was his belief that it could cure almost anything, and he was a major force behind the popular notion that cocaine was a cure for morphine addiction. Of course, this situation was to end in tragedy many times. One noteworthy case was with that of Sigmund Freud's longtime friend and colleague, Ernst Fleischl von Maxow.

As so many in his day Ernst Fleischl von Maxow was addicted to morphine. Freud, believing in cocaine's ability to cure anything, prescribed it to his good friend Ernst. It is certain this only compounded his problems. Yet Freud could not accept that his pet cure-all was not working. He blamed von Maxow for having a weak will. After Freud had prescribed several dose increases his unfortunate patient slipped into delirium and finally died. Freud refused to accept any responsibility for his friend's death and remained unshaken in his belief in the effectiveness of the cocaine treatment.

One of the strangest and most disturbing aspects of Freud's work was his theory of personality development. Here is a sad irony of Freud's work because he was almost certainly on the right track. But again he was derailed by his bizarre obsessions, his extreme impressionability and his undying belief in the correctness of his ideas.

It is strange indeed that a man as intelligent as Sigmund Freud was so easily impressed by some of the things he was so drawn to. A prime example is the effects the play "King

Oedipus" had on Freud. He saw this play early in his adult life and it altered his perception of the world and colored his thinking from that point on. Freud, already confused by unnatural sexual feelings for his mother, was moved to develop his famous Oedipus complex. Freud used himself as a template, then projected his own personal neurotic idiosyncrasies onto his patients and finally onto the entire human population. In advocating such nonsense as infantile sexuality, Freud exposes his own personality dysfunction. That he applied his convoluted thinking to something as important as personality development and the subconscious is the real pity. The revolutionary concept of the subconscious became entangled with his neurotic nonsense of repression. This mix of a legitimate theory and his perverted sexual feelings for his mother would spawn the ground work for the "False Memory Syndrome" craze of the 20th century. The tragedy of being falsely accused of sexually abusing children would befall thousands and was only possible because of Freud's theory of memory repression and his own perverted feeling towards his mother.

Other detractors point to Freud's relationship to his patients. It seems that all of Freud's patients were young, attractive wealthy women. Freud himself writes, "I cannot imagine bringing myself to delve into the psychical mechanism of hysteria in anyone who struck me as low-minded and repellent." He explicitly blamed hysteria on "precocious experience of sexual relations with actual excitement of the genitals, resulting from sexual abuse." He was convinced that female masturbation caused hysteria.

Where Freud got his idea's one can only guess, but there is no denying that he was obsessed with sex.

Consider for a moment, Dr. Freud (a trusted psychiatrist) in his office, nose full of cocaine, (for his "nasal reflex" of course) discussing hysteria and female masturbation with some attractive, young woman who is also high on cocaine. It is not hard to imagine what conflict of interest might arise. By our standards today such a scenario seems absurd, yet it was a common setting for Sigmund Freud.

Freud's theory of personality development, repression and the subconscious, his concepts such as division in the psyche and infantile sexuality, and by his own admission, sexual feelings for his mother, force us to consider Mrs. Thornton's allegations that cocaine had indeed played a part in influencing Freud's thinking.

But the most damning aspect of Freud's work is his theory of repression and his obsession with incest. The mythology that developed from Freud's theory of repressed memories contributed directly to the False Memory Syndrome craze of the 20th century and has destroyed many lives.

Conclusion

When Sigmund Freud's work, theories, methodology and ethics are taken fully into consideration, it's hard not to wince. It seems the history of psychiatry is not without a sense of irony.

Sigmund Freud, a man obsessed with sex who used and freely distributed a dangerous drug, a man who refused to accept responsibility for killing several people, including a close friend, a man who's ethical conduct would land him in prison today, a man whose work has caused such suffering... This is our Father of psychoanalysis.

Sources Used

Freud, Sigmund, <u>Standard Edition of the Complete Psychological Works of Sigmund Freud</u>

Greenbaum, Adolf, <u>Foundations of Psychoanalysis</u>

Haberman, Viktor J., <u>A Criticism of Psychoanalysis</u> (Journal of Abnormal Psychology)

Hodgson, Barbara, <u>In the Arms of Morpheus</u>

Pendergrast, Mark, <u>Victims of Memory</u>

Shorter, Edward, <u>A History of Psychiatry</u>

Thornton, E. M., <u>Freudian Fallacy</u>

Woods, Garth, <u>Myth of Neurosis</u>

Yates, Frances, <u>The Art of Memory</u>

Extreme Communications

Matthew tried to hear Master Kim's words. Tried to feel as he felt in Master Kim's presence. "Never react out of fear or anger . . ." But this was not an exercise in the dojo. This was not a controlled engagement, it was for real. These were real thugs. Street hoods, not his fellow students acting as aggressors. The one facing him now outweighed him by, what . . . thirty pounds? And there was the knife.

He made a conscious effort to control his breathing. As he did a fact came into sharp focus. He had never tested his martial skills under real conditions. He thought of the upcoming test for his black belt. He had been assured by many that to earn a black belt from Master Kim Jong he would get bruised - several times.

As apprehensive as he was about facing the master in a real fight, this was different. Much different. Matthew remembered his green belt. Master Kim had promised him, "One of my green belts fight good. Very good." He had one eye almost closed and a near dislocated wrist as a result of his green belt test - not to mention how he hurt after earning his brown belt. He wondered at his anxiety over this fellow facing him now. When once a fellow student asked Master Kim about what to do in such a situation he answered, "give as much consideration as time will allow."

The sound of the fellow asking something about money while brandishing the knife barely registered as he tried to follow Master Kim's instructions. Consider . . . as much as time allows. He noticed his adversary had a weak chin. He was also missing a tooth. He stood slouching as if his back hurt. The other fellow – about his size – looked nervous, as if he had had too much coffee. Matthew remembered the multiple attacker exercise: address the most immediate threat first. This would be the big guy with the knife, who was repeating his demand for payment. From the back of his mind Master Kim spoke, "honest words transcend evil intentions" . . . Matt found his voice, "I'll not give you anything. I am well prepared to defend myself." Matt stepped back into an open stance. There was silence.

The big guy had a puzzled look on his face. He looked to his left to ask his cohort if he had heard correctly. Matt noticed he had taken his eyes completely off him. A show of disrespect to a martial artist, a fatal mistake in a street fight.

Matt had an urge to fire a front kick into his groin. Then he heard Master Kim again, "Ah Matt-u, Thucydides say, of all manifestations of power, restraint impresses men most." And while Matt doubted this fellow had even heard of Thucydides, he realized his breathing had slowed considerably. He also imagined how this fellow lost his tooth. Matt noticed movement as the smaller of the two stepped away. It was then he noticed the guy was armed with a length of pipe. So they were both armed. This perhaps changed things.

He was aware of the big guy speaking again, this time the words "fuck you up" registered loud and clear. As if almost by cue he heard Master Kim, "Confidence and courage far out-weigh cowardly boasting."

As if he was hearing someone else say it Matt heard himself answer, "Try it you big buffoon, see what happens".

The big guy took a step towards Matt. He responded by assuming a Kwon Boxing stance. The big guy stopped at what he thought was a safe distance. Holding the knife out trying to threaten, he snidely remarked, "You think you Kung Fu or some'n". Matt noticed a slight trembling of the knife. He saw doubt in the big man's eyes.

"Ah Matt-u eyes, window of soul."

Matt's words seem to come from inside. "I am a student of Master Kim Jong."

The big guy again looked at his partner in crime. "Ain't that the gook who fucked big Burnie up?"

Before he could answer Matt found himself speaking. "Mr. Jong is a master of Korean martial arts, he is an honorable man. I advise you to speak respectfully or I'll . . ."

The big guy was taken aback by the fact that Matt had closed the distance between them. In an overreaction to this he stepped back, stumbling backward as he did.

The big guy's question sparked Matthew's memory. A newspaper article, "Would-be Rapist Hospitalized by Local Martial Arts Instructor." In fact it was this story that brought Matthew to Master Kim Jong's, Hwa Rang Do studio. He remembered how impressed he had been with the witnesses' descriptions of the confrontation. He also remembered how repulsed he had been by the character of the big Burnie fellow.

Burnis Hargrove, ex-heavy weight boxer, three-time loser, drug addict, sex offender. One of those who seem to continually fall through the cracks. Mr. Hargrove's luck ran out when he put his hands on young Linda Jong. Had big Burnie not been high on PCP, it's likely that Master Kim would not have broken an arm . . . dislocated his shoulder . . . smashed a knee cap . . . gouged out an eye . . . and fractured his skull. But the big man couldn't get enough.

Matt was brought from his memories by the smaller guy's voice, "Say Spike, lets don't mess with this Jap hocus pocus - its bad man". The big guy looked from Matt, to his cohort, back to Matt, his uncertainty was painfully obvious. The Master's words again came to Matthew. "Always remember Matt-u, an attacker must win, the vanquished must only survive." Could he avoid this confrontation? His martial arts philosophy required him to do so if possible. He knew Master Jong would not accept an insult as an excuse for fighting. "Matt-u, Hwa Rang Do code, better to accept insult than risk danger, better to risk danger, than injury, better to injure than to maim, better to maim than to kill, better to kill than to be killed. Each man must decide for himself . . ."

The master's words were cut short.

The big guy stepped forward, teeth clinched. In one fluid motion Matt fired a front kick into the big man's groin. The big guy bent at the waist as if suddenly violently ill and vomiting. His knife wielding arm extended, was an easy mark. Over and back. The knife rattled as it hit the pavement.

As if in slow motion the smaller of the two raised the length of pipe over his head. Matt felt the side kick start in his shoulders, the motion traveling through his body, his hips picking up the momentum, his left leg firing out. Textbook in its execution, the extension was perfect. He was barely aware of the resistance offered by the guy's solar plexus. The kick lifted the attacker off his feet sending him several yards through the air. He landed squarely on his back, his wind knocked from his lungs.

Matt stood there. He heard Master Kim's voice, "Matt-u, had you good cause to risk such danger?" He was startled. This time the voice was real. He turned to see Master Kim standing a few feet behind him.

He assumed the respect-stance, bowed at the waist. "Sensei." Master Kim bowed slightly in response. "Forgive me Sensei, after all your teaching I allowed myself to react out of anger."

Master Kim looked into Matthew's eyes and without his lips moving he clearly heard his words, "Ah Matt-u, sticks and stones . . ."

Matthew's bottom jaw dropped. He realized the old legend of a Hwa Rang Do master, being able to project his thought telepathically was fact. All he could do was utter, "Master Kim."

Master Kim smiled. "Come Matt-u, you have much to learn." The moment was broken by the sudden moaning of the big guy suffering from his dislocated shoulder.

Matthew looked around and asked, "Master Kim, what about them"?

"Ah Matt-u, they have much to learn as well . . ."

Could Have Been Me

As Charlie checked the Jiffy Mart from the phone booth something caught his eye. A large moth stood out among the many smaller night insects buzzing the neon light of the electronic bug zapper that hung on a hook by the door. The larger moth among the smaller insects held significance for Charlie. He watched the moth as it flew in random circles, both envying and hating it for its size.

Charlie had suffered from "Little man's complex" all his life. He wasn't small enough to have little man's complex, he just did. He had liked being a bully and that had gotten him beaten up several times. He still tried, but was much more selective with the people he chose to bully. But he never lost an opportunity to prove to himself or other people that he was tough or smart or fast or any number of things he wasn't, but wished so much he was. Like so many bullies, Charlie was the product of a dysfunctional home. His abuse hadn't been so much physical as emotional.

After his psychotic mother had done her work, she had left young Charlie on the doorstep of her psychotic sister to complete this masterpiece. This was when Charlie was just starting school. A year or two later Charlie's younger brother Wayne was dropped at the same doorstep.

As Charlie watched the large moth his mind momentarily relived his past and was conscious of the weight in his coat pocket. He thought of old Leonard who had been here at the Jiffy Mart for as long as he could remember. He tried to imagine the look on the old man's face when he announced his intentions. He pulled the pistol from his coat pocket and looked at it again, a .38 caliber. Charlie didn't know the make or model, all he knew was that when he had it he had the power of life and death in his hands. Only a "Big" man had such power.

When Charlie had paroled the first time he was sure people would respect him because of the many tattoos he had. He acted as he did before, people responded as they had before. When he paroled the second time, with more tattoos, he was even surer people would respect him. Surely someone of his experience was to be respected. Charlie was dumbfounded to learn that children and little old ladies were the only ones who showed something even close to what he considered respect. He just could not grasp why people did not show him proper respect.

Of course after Charlie's early childhood and first twenty years of adult life, his thinking was so distorted that he could no longer grasp what real respect was. The concept of fear and respect were hopelessly confused in his mind. Was it the rejection he had experienced from his Mother? Was it the abuse he suffered at the hands of the Aunt who raised him? Was it something from prison? No one knew. Charlie had driven away every friend he had ever had. Everyone made him feel like a nobody. He noticed movement at the door of the Jiffy Mart. A customer was leaving. It was time and soon old Leonard would know he was somebody!

He told himself that if the old man made one smart ass remark he would shoot him on the spot. The old man had already shown a marked lack of respect. Leonard had no right to be as cocky as he was. Why he was hardly bigger then Charlie and had to be pushing seventy. Like the day he had ejected the shoplifters. The two young thugs had underestimated the old man and thought they could easily intimidate him. When one of the thugs reached out to grab Leonard's shirt sleeve, he fired a short jab that landed squarely on the chin of the young thief. The fellow hit the floor and as he was regaining his senses, Leonard retrieved the stolen merchandise and calmly placed it back on the shelf. Then as the downed thug's partner in crime stood looking on stunned, Leonard slapped him up-side the head and told them, "You young punks get outta here before the cops come." Charlie stood and thought for a moment, "If he had done me like that." His thoughts trailed off as he felt apprehension swell up inside. "I'm not afraid of that old fucker" He realized he had said this aloud. He looked at the revolver again; it was time to do it.

The isolated location of the Jiffy Mart seemed to make it an ideal mark. The fact that his residence was only two miles away didn't seem to be an obstacle to his plan for quick money. Like so many before him Charlie did not learn from his mistakes and so was bound to repeat them.

As Charlie neared the entrance of the store, he noticed the old man had removed his shirt. In his tank top style undershirt his numerous tattoos were visible under the florescent lights of the store. So this was why the old man always wore long sleeves, what people said about old Leonard might be true. He found himself stopped at the front door. Then his heart skipped a beat as the old man looked directly at him. Seconds passed. Charlie could hear his heart beating in his ears. His mind raced. The old coot just stared at him, then turned away and returned to the mundane task of closing up.

Charlie pushed ever so lightly on the door. The bolt rattled in its housing. The door was locked. He felt relief. Then he cussed the old man under his breath. "You're a lucky old fucker, Leonard. I'm not one of those young cowards you pulled your shit on." He stood there looking down the road and thought of his leaky frame house only two miles away. He fumed at his inheritance. He should have been given more land. Instead he was given only a few acres and a leaky frame house. His brother, Wayne had always been favored, he was always pampered, and the fucker was always … Charlie was startled by a rattling. Before he could snap to old Leonard was standing before him asking, "You need something kid?" He stood frozen staring at the old man.

"Well sonny, if you need something you better say something cuz I'm closing."

Charlie's thoughts were confused and he felt a lump in his throat. More time passed as he felt sweat beads breaking out all over his body.

"I'm forty one, old man." There. He had spoken defiantly to Leonard, he wasn't afraid of this old man.

The old man's eyes squinted producing a deep set of crow's feet at each temple. "Listen son, I don't give a doodly-squat how old you are. You either gonna buy something and damn fast, or I'm lockin the door." The old man's stare intensified.

"Uh, yeah, uh . . . some beer." Charlie stood frozen. Old Leonard looked him up and down, his eyes stopping for a moment at the bulge in his jacket pocket. He knew. Somehow old Leonard knew.

Leonard stepped back and held the door. "Well I don't deliver, hurry your ass up." Charlie stepped in as if walking through a minefield. He walked to the cooler, retrieved a six pack without noticing the brand. His mind was racing. As he set the six pack on the counter the old man leaned over and asked, "Just what the hell are you up to buy'n beer at this late hour sonny boy, and some light-ass beer you got there." Leonard drilled in with a look that made Charlie's blood run cold. Charlie was caught off guard by Leonard's statement. As he reached his hand into his coat pocket the old man held up both hands in a gesture to wait.

"Before you do something real stupid, let me tell you something, Charlie. I knew your momma and your aunt. I know you been battered around and it's left some marks on you. Hell, we all got marks left on us from our rais'n. I know you been in some trouble Charlie, and if I guess right, you probably got some more marks from that. Still Charlie, you ain't got it half bad. A little land, a house, hell of a lot more'n I ever had. As long as you don't show me that, whatever it is you got stashed in your jacket pocket, I can sell you this friggen soda you call beer and forget this. But you pull a god damn gun on me and I swear I'll either whip your ass or make you kill me. Either way, there ain't a chance in hell of you get'n away with this cause I ain't given you a mother scratch'n dime, not willingly I won't! So make up your mind. And do it now sonny boy."

Charlie was trembling so bad he couldn't conceal it. At that moment car lights flooded the store entrance. As if Leonard's lecture wasn't bad enough now a lawman had to show up. A damned county law man. A big uniformed officer struggled out of the squad car and lumbered towards the front door.

Charlie stood frozen as he watched the officer near. The big officer pushed the door open and asked, "You still opened Leonard?" As he stood in the doorway he shot a cold stare at Charlie.

"Yeah flat foot, may as well. I'm wait'n on this snot-nose kid already." Charlie laid a ten dollar bill on the counter. The big officer stopped for a moment and looked down at him.

"You out late aren't you, got some identification?" Leonard cut in quickly, "Yeah he got identification. He just showed it to me, for this here six pack." Leonard nodded at the six pack and the officer looked down at it and frowned.

"Always a smart-ass, aren't you Leonard? Learn that in prison?"

"What I learned in prison is my business, ok fat ass?" Leonard squinted at the officer.

"What I learned since I been out is that we ain't got no god damned curfew. You rousting my customers is real bad for business and I don't have that many. So if you please. Hurry your big ass up so I can close."

"Ok, ok. Shit Leonard, I ought to arrest your ass, you ornery old bastard."

"Well hell, its ten minutes after one and I still got a snot nosed punk and a fat ass cop mill'n around in here, ya'll got one minute and I lock ya'll up in here!"

At this, Charlie hurried out without collecting his change. As he pushed open the door he noticed the big moth on the sidewalk. It writhed around, it's wings scorched from the bug zapper. He stared at it for a moment then took the time to crush it under foot.

The big officer set a large bag of chips and several candy bars on the counter.

"That guy is trouble Leonard, why you want to make his bond? And don't say that wasn't what you were doing because I know better".

"Was a time they said that about me." The big officer laughed out loud, "Hell Leonard, you were trouble!"

"Yeah, and I could of used someone to make my bond a few times".

"Isn't that old Minnie Preston's nephew?" Leonard looked up at the officer and spoke.

"Yeah, that's him. Minnie and his Mom is why that boy is so fucked up. They were both nutty as shit house rats. What you expect to come from that kind of a set up?"

The big cop reflected for a moment then spoke, "Yeah Leonard, that's true, but the boy never wanted for anything. Hell he wasn't ever hungry." Leonard gave him another of his looks and the crow's feet at his temples became deeper than the cop had ever seen them.

"Well I tell yah, there are things that can eat at a man more'n be'n hungry or wet. Things you can't see right out. I don't spect you to understand. Like when a man needs a drink more'n something to eat. If you ain't never had thoughts that trouble you more than an empty belly ... well you can't understand what shit Charlie's been through".

"And what about you Leonard, hell what I hear you had less than Charlie, that what made you so mean?" Leonard got quiet for a moment or two.

"Least I had a Dad. Mean as hell it's true, but he wasn't crazy, least wise not like Minnie and that bitch of a Mom of Charlie's. Least he taught me some man stuff, to hunt, to work, to stud up under pressure. That's the only way I made it thru prison".

The big county officer stared out the glass front door and drug his huge hand over his five o'clock shadow as he pondered Leonard's words.

"I suppose that was a tough time for you, long as you were there Leonard".

"No worse'n Nam. But that's part of what I'm try'n to get through that thick noggin of yore, I had some prepare'n, didn't just get thrown into it. Not like Charlie did, and I guaran-god damn-tee-yah it makes one hell of a difference"

The big county officer paid for his chips, "I don't know Leonard, either way it's kind of a shame".

The door came almost off its hinges. Not because Charlie was a powerful kicker, but because it was so old and dilapidated. He flung the six pack of grape soda he had mistaken for beer against the wall. The stray mutt that he had subjugated and had been abusing for the last two months ran for the couch. After scurrying under the couch she poked her snout out looking up at her master as only a loyal dog can do.

"That old bastard!"

Charlie felt as if his brain would explode with rage. "I should have shot that old fucker and the cop both". He kicked at the coffee table sending it flying through the air. He leaned over and called to the shaggy mutt. She came hugging the floor her tail between her legs. As Charlie looked down at the dog it was as if he saw something of himself in the poor beast. He looked down at the quivering mass and for a moment felt pity. But Charlie's old friends, anger, hatred and bitterness came rushing in on him and he was forced to lash out at whatever he could.

He buried the toe of his boot into the dog's side, sending it into the corner with several broken ribs. It was then Charlie noticed the small mound in the floor. In a complete rage now, he had lost all control.

"You shit in the floor again!" The mutt was trying to get to her feet when Charlie pulled the revolver from his jacket pocket. In a mindless state, he leveled the front sight on the dog. "Die you bitch!" One shot, a second, a third, six in all, the shots echoing in the darkness.

The first round knocked a tuft of fur from the mutt's hip, the force spinning the animal around, the exiting bullet splattering the water stained sheet rock with blood. The second round clipped the dog's foreleg, almost severing it. The third round hitting low in the rib cage, knocking the dog to the floor. The fourth round struck the floor well in front of the animal sending splinters of wood and old flooring into the air. The fifth round struck the shoulder at a sharp angle glancing away, sending more fur into the air.

The mutt lay bleeding profusely as fibers of dog hair slowly drifted down thru the slightly visible vapors of burnt gun powder. Charlie then kicked at the bleeding, whimpering animal.

Leonard opened the store at 7:00 a.m. as he had done for years. He had just opened the front door when the big county officer pulled up. He again lumbered his way into the Jiffy Mart. "Say Leonard, did you hear about Minnie Preston's nephew? That thug that was in here last night, he tore up the old house that Minnie left him, and then shot some old dog he had, and then he blew his brains out." Leonard didn't acknowledge.

"A constable thought he heard a shot and went to check it out. They place the time at about 2:00 AM."

Leonard looked up at the big officer with his usual cold stare, the crow's feet at his temples deepening.

"Hell Leonard it could have been you got shot."

"You're right cop, it could have been me …"

A Note on Foolishness and Terror

It was the spring of 1974. The new horror film, "The Exorcist" was in its thirteenth week at the Wilshire Theater in Mesquite, Texas – the last showing of the uncut version.

This story is as much about my friend Larry as it is the disaster that follows. As were most all of my friends at that time, Larry was a party animal. I prefer that term to rampant abusers of drugs and alcohol. Nonetheless, the latter term was more accurate and of all the abusers, Larry was the most rampant. He had this odd idiosyncrasy... if he was unimpaired enough to still function, more dope was needed. Making a spectacle of himself and whoever he was with in public was his favorite sport. While any other "high freak" would struggle to maintain a low profile in public, Larry would go out of his way to see this was impossible. Not too many people went anywhere in public with Larry while high more than once.

Earlier in the week we had discussed going to see some new movie that my crazy friend, Larry was so excited about. He showed up at my apartment that ill-fated day babbling about a surprise. He unfolded a single square of toilet paper to reveal a small blue speck. He carefully toyed with this "speck" and I realized it was many tiny blue specks. One hundred hits of "Blue Microdot" he called it. A single dose was smaller than a pinhead. He was told it was the best acid he would ever do. It was the smallest drug related thing I had ever seen.

He offered me one, which I foolishly accepted and when I crunched it, I caught a slight bitter taste, not LSD . . . What then?

"Larry-boy, this shit has taste, how many times I got to tell you, LSD is tasteless"

"Man this is the best acid you will ever do!"

"Yeah, says who? Where did you get it?" I leaned over slightly looking down my nose at him.

"Ronny Phillips, he just got a thousand hits and if it is as good as he says it is I'm going back and buy all he will sell me, at least another hundred".

"Ha Ha, Ronny Phillips, figures, he is the only egg head goofier about dope than you. At least he knows his drugs; we know we will get off".

We had planned to ingest our party favor, drive directly to the theater, catch the 3:00PM showing and hopefully spare me being high on LSD and trapped in public with "head case Larry" for too long. Not to be!

My common-law date had to do what women do when men are in a hurry. So we smoked a joint and guzzled several beers. When we arrived we were over an hour late and the first effects of the "Blue Microdot" were already closing in on us as we entered the lobby of the theater.

It started out like LSD, a pleasantly stimulating, euphoric feeling of giddiness. But this had a strange numbness to it, also a kind of throbbing in the temples. Sounds and voices had a ring to them and seemed amplified. I was feeling real strange standing around the lobby so at one point I went to the men's room and when I entered it was as if I left one dimension and entered another. Larry followed a short time later and when he entered I was standing in front of the mirror staring at myself in wonder. My face had a mottled look to it, both flushed and blushing at the same time – a pattern of shifting colors. The pupils of my eyes were so dilated they were without color. I turned and looked at Larry and his eyes and face looked the same.

"Larry, look at your face, look at our faces, what is this shit. We can't go out there looking like this". Larry just looked at himself and laughed. It was kind of funny. I noticed that this stuff didn't make one laugh uncontrollably as most good LSD does. And, the fact that Larry wasn't the usual clown was odd, almost unsettling.

Then all of a sudden I became aware of the tracers. Otherwise known as the "Strobe effect", an optical illusion where a moving object is followed by a train of several or dozens of image copies trailing after. "Wow".

Larry looked at me as I swooshed my hand back and forth in front of my face. He laughed,

"Good tracers, huh?" I had never seen such vivid tracers. They were even evident in my peripheral vision. A bit of a distraction, but even more distracting was the fact that I was starting to see "floaters." Floaters: the rupture of microscopic capillaries in the neural retina and dead receptor cells in the vitreous humor that causes visual anomalies on the cornea. These appear as small fibers floating harmlessly through the plane of vision. But for one under the influence of LSD, they can appear as anything from Timothy Leary's "spirits" to Hunter S. Thompson's "bats". To me they looked like transparent alien symbols floating across my field of vision. Without realizing I was speaking out loud I mumbled something like, "This is some real strange shit Larry".

We had lost track of time and the previous showing was turning out. We re-entered the lobby and the walls were breathing heavily. I heard Larry behind me carrying on about something, asking about how I was getting off, I think. He was always obsessed with how high other people were and it was starting to get on my nerves because I was having difficulty concentrating on more than one thing at a time, which for now it was ignoring him and finding our way to some seats.

As we happened by the exit aisle a crowd of people with blank faces shuffled past. Not a word was uttered from the passing movie goers. Then I was struck by a fact: the people in the crowd had the same mottled pallor I had noticed on my own face. I thought to myself, "There must be a lot of this 'Blue Microdot' in town, or that was one hell of a movie". If I only had known.

From behind me someone asked, "So how was the movie?" No answer. The procession continued on in silence. Larry and I looked at each other. Slowly the entire crowd cleared without a single word and I noticed that others were watching the silent crowd pass with puzzled looks.

By the time the movie started my date was worried about me. She asked if I was okay.

I asked her, "Yeah sure, why do you ask?" She told me she thought my face looked strange. I would have been surprised if it hadn't, considering how I was feeling. Suddenly on the screen appeared the perverted statue of the Virgin Mary with its bloody mutant protrusions. I felt a deep revulsion. I turned to Larry and demanded to know what I had just seen.

He laughed and said, "I'm not really sure, just keep watching." My date was shocked and could tell that I was as well and asked me if I wanted to leave. At some point I decided to watch the entire film . . . no matter what.

Sometime later Larry got up to go to the snack bar. While he was gone the devil took full possession of the girl, flailing her around on the bed in the infamous and revolting scene where her neck inflates. For anyone who has not experienced the loss of reality from the use of LSD, or the utter sickness of the uncut version of The Exorcist, description is difficult. And to describe experiencing these two unnatural events simultaneously is impossible. My heart was literally "in my throat" and I lost my ability to breathe for several seconds. Just as I was regaining my breath, Larry appeared. I collared him roughly and shook him accusing him of cowardice until my date and an usher made me sit.

At this point my date begged me to reconsider leaving. Why I continued to subject myself to this spiritual torture, I have no answer.

What is the clinical definition of insanity? It didn't matter at this point. I know I was very close. From that point on, watching was a tremendous struggle. The blasphemous cursing and spewing of vomit and blood insulted not just my intelligence, but my spirit. My soul sickened as the story continued. At one point I noticed an older effeminate looking fellow several seats to my right. He held a handkerchief to his mouth with white knuckles, his eyes frozen in abject terror! I was struck with a strange notion, "He is as frightened as I am." As the horror continued I felt my soul being irrevocably scarred. I sat through the vomiting, blaspheming and senseless vile cursing, thinking it would never end. It seemed it just went on and on and on. I found myself tensing up every time the camera drew closer to that damned bedroom door where the girl was.

I was distracted from this hellish onslaught by a walkie-talkie. I looked around and the fellow with the handkerchief was being helped into a wheelchair by two paramedics. I thought to myself, "You bastard, you die in here and it's a one way ticket to hell . . ." Still, I thought him lucky, he was leaving. I turned back to the film wondering to myself why I didn't just follow them out.

It finally ended. Thank God! As we filed out of the theater to the lobby, Larry's voice was the only one I heard, and I wished I couldn't hear him. I was already blaming him for what I had just experienced. Despite the fact that everyone else was dead quiet and my physical ears could have heard a pin drop, it was as if I had ten thousand caged demons screaming in my head. As we slowly shuffled along and I realized that the only sounds I could hear were not real ones, I reflected back to seeing the earlier showing turn out and how quiet they were and the expressions they wore. I understood then. As we entered the light of the lobby I had a definite feeling of having escaped.

Like acting in a replay of watching the earlier showing turn out, anxious faces were looking on asking, "Was it good … Was it scary?"

No one answered. As a single stunned body we all shuffled slowly toward the fresh air of the early spring night. Finally someone spoke up as if frustrated by our collective silence.

"Well how was it . . .?" At this I felt some strange responsibility and to this day cannot account for why I did it. I stepped into the open and faced the on-looking crowd. I heard myself cry out almost at the top of my lungs, "Don't go in there if you're tripping!" I stood for several seconds exchanging glances with individuals in the crowd. It is impossible to describe what passed between us, and in remembering I ask myself if I believe it, and have no answer. As I felt hot tears running down my cheeks I saw several people turn and leave the theater. I did gain some small measure of redemption by trying to spare those people from entering the hell I had so willingly plunged into.

Aftermath

Needless to say my next many nights were very restless. My wife-to-be and I didn't speak for days and few were the times we spoke of this night in the next twenty-two years of marriage. I would not talk to Larry for months, wouldn't even let him come around. I know I entered that theater willingly, but someone had to bear the guilt for what I had suffered and all this was Larry's idea. I finally began the slow process of putting this experience behind me. I found it somewhat therapeutic in analyzing and doing various research on different aspects of what, exactly, I had experienced.

Later I realized that before that night I had never actually heard the term, "Exorcist". I learned from our good friend, Ronny Phillips that some wildcat chemist was producing STP, a drug several times more potent than LSD, and selling it as "Blue Microdot." Ronny continued to use it and wound up in a nut house somewhere. Larry finally drove himself into the gutter with his incessant drug abuse. Not long after our night at the movies he was in therapy. The last I heard he was in a nut house too. I read in the Dallas Times Herald that an Albert Wriggle suffered a stroke during the last uncut showing of The

Exorcist at the Wilshire Theater. Mr. Wriggle later died at Parkland Hospital. No telling where he wound up. It took me over a year to come to grips with that experience and I am still occasionally haunted by the events of that day.

Small Green Tree Lizard

As time passes, I only miss you more. The farther away you go, the closer I feel to you.

I can no longer deny I love you . . . my denial has become such a farce, that for me to even think it, is a poignant reminder of how hopeless my case is.

Completely lost to me now, you continue to haunt my existence.

As I feel the wind on my face, I see it in your hair. That beautiful raven hair, that is surely graying by now . . .

Graying, as mine is, as this time passes. As time passes . . . without you.

I have robbed myself of the wondrous pleasure of growing old with you.

My aging is no longer a mark of how long I have lived, but a mark of how long I have been without you.

At night I look skyward to the stars. I stand alone under them and wonder . . . Can you see these same stars?